DINOSAUR

BREAKOUT

DINOSAUR BREAKOUT

JUDITH SILVERTHORNE

Edited by Barbara Sapergia.
Cover illustrations by Aries Cheung.
Cover and book design by Duncan Campbell.
Printed and bound in Canada at Gauvin Press.

National Library of Canada Cataloguing in Publication Data

Silverthorne, Judith, date-
Dinosaur breakout / Judith Silverthorne.

ISBN 1-55050-294-8

I. Title.

PS8587.I2763D55 2004 jC813'.54 C2004-901621-0

10 9 8 7 6 5 4 3 2

2517 Victoria Avenue
Regina, Saskatchewan
Canada S4P 0T2

available in Canada and the US from:
Fitzhenry & Whiteside
195 Allstate Parkway
Markham, Ontario
Canada L3R 4T8

The publisher gratefully acknowledges the financial assistance of the Saskatchewan Arts Board, the Canada Council for the Arts, including the Millennium Arts Fund, the Government of Canada through the Book Publishing Industry Development Program (BPIDP), and the City of Regina Arts Commission, for its publishing program.

As ever, for Aaron,
my son, and my inspiration on dinosaurs

And for all of my nieces, a nephew, and their families

In Canada:
Michelle & Scott: Emma, Tyson
Christine & Ryan: Kelsey, Elaina
Amanda; Amie; Grant

In New Zealand:
Tayla; Zara; Shania

CHAPTER ONE

Something big and dark moved within the small bluff of trees at the bottom of a hill just ahead of Daniel. He stopped and stared. But nothing moved! The only sounds were the light rustling of leaves and the swish of long summer grasses at his feet. Then the cawing of a crow far overhead in the bright sunlight urged him forward.

He headed across the gentle rises of the land above the Frenchman River Valley in the southwest area of Saskatchewan. Behind him lay the Bringham family farm home, where he'd lived since he'd been born twelve years earlier. Although the farm was situated on reasonably flat land near the top of a valley, the pasture gave way to undulating hills, and ahead of him, the land would soon plunge into steeper inclines until it reached the valley floor.

He was on his way to his secret hideout, in a coulee at the base of two hills near the edge of the family's west quarter of pastureland. He hadn't been there for several weeks, and now that school was out for the summer holidays, this would be the only chance to go for a while. He'd soon be kept busy helping his family run their dinosaur dig tourist operation. This would be their first year of enterprise since their neighbour, Ole Pederson, had found the full skeletal remains of an *Edmontosaurus* on his property. He had formed a business deal with Daniel's family and the neighbouring Lindstroms and everyone was busy preparing for opening day.

Ahead of Daniel, the dry greenish-brown landscape was dotted with clumps of pale green foliage, patches of wildflowers, yellow bunches of sweet clover, and a myriad of grasses and weeds. All of them gave off their own distinct aromas as Daniel brushed by them, especially the abundant sage. As he approached, startled gophers darted into their holes, their squeaks piercing the steady drone of insects about their daily forages.

Daniel quickened his pace through the ravine to the bottom of the hill, circling the stand of trees. He stopped short. There had been another flash of something moving! Something too large to be Dactyl. Besides, his golden retriever had disappeared over the hills ages before, dive-bombing after a rabbit. Dactyl stayed true to his nature and namesake, the *Pterodactyl.*

"Who's there?" He listened carefully. No response. "Is anyone there?" Nothing.

He shook his head and turned along the coulee that

led to his hideout. *Snap!* The little hairs on the back of his neck bristled. The sound came from the trees behind him, as if something, or someone, had stepped on some dry twigs. Daniel took a quick breath and veered to his right, in the opposite direction from his hideout, pretending he'd intended on going that way all along.

He had no intention of letting any outsiders know the location of his secret hideout. It was his special place, where he housed his private dinosaur fossils and rocks, and he had some important business to take care of, which he wanted to do away from prying eyes.

"Dactyl! Here, boy! Dactyl!" he called urgently, but no answering bark came. Someone must be following him! He was sure there were no large, dangerous animals lurking anywhere around the district.

Daniel felt his stomach muscles tighten. He had to discover who was out there! Ever since he and his neighbour, Ole Pederson, had revealed their dinosaur findings and the adventures they'd had a year and a half earlier, the location of Daniel's hideout had been a target for speculation. Especially with the kids from school.

Daniel had made his best friend, Jed Lindstrom, promise to keep quiet about its whereabouts. But it was only a matter of time before Jed let the information slip accidentally. His whole family had a habit of blurting out confidences without thinking. The good thing was that Jed was directionally challenged and wouldn't be able to find it easily again on his own. He couldn't find his way out of a potato gunnysack unless someone led him. And he'd only been to Daniel's hideout once. But Daniel didn't trust the Nelwin brothers, the school bullies.

He had to lose whoever was behind him, and fast. Suddenly, he spotted a pile of rocks a couple of metres up a hillside. Quickly, he headed towards them, weaving this way and that as if he were searching for something on the ground. At one point, he picked up a small round stone. Then, making sure no one could see him from below, he ducked behind the outcropping. Adjusting his backpack into a more comfortable position, he crouched and waited.

Moments later, he heard the scuffling of hurrying feet coming towards him. His heart thumped rapidly inside his chest. He tried to slow his breathing and not make a sound. His legs stiffened and he readied to leap with the stone in his hand. As the scuffling came closer, he recalled his first meeting with old man Pederson. What if the person following him was huge and strong? Maybe he'd be better off hiding instead of attacking, until he knew what he was up against.

The footsteps slowed and Daniel eased himself farther behind the outcropping of rocks, as quiet as his cat Marble waiting for a bird to land within pouncing distance. Just as he thought the person was going to stop and search his hiding place, the footsteps accelerated past him. Daniel waited a few moments until he judged them far enough away, then peeked around the edge.

Craig Nelwin! He'd know him anywhere. Whew! That was a close one! Daniel eased himself onto his knees and waited for him to disappear. Craig was a beefy fifteen-year-old bent on making the world revolve around his whims. He had repeated Grade Eight classes this past year and had a perpetual chip on his shoulder. He also seemed bent on taking any of his problems out on Daniel. Especially since Daniel had become famous locally for his part in the recent dinosaur discoveries in the area. It was odd, though, that Craig's older brother, Todd, wasn't with him. The one rarely went anywhere without the other.

Daniel brushed the rock dust off his pants and walked around the stone pile. A solid body blocked his way. *Todd.* The tall, chunky sixteen-year-old, muscular from heaving bales, was no one to tangle with! Daniel gulped. Todd's brooding eyes glared at him from his sneering face.

"Think you're pretty smart, eh, Dino boy?" Todd shoved him backwards with his meaty hands. He was bigger and meaner than his brother.

Daniel braced his feet and stood his ground, clutching the stone in his hand.

"I don't know what you mean." Daniel tried to brush past him, but Todd gave him a harder shove.

This time Daniel slid backwards and he reached frantically to grab hold of the rocks. Before he connected, Todd slammed his huge hands into Daniel's chest again. Suddenly, from behind, Daniel's feet were kicked out from under him. He toppled backwards. Craig had returned!

Daniel felt himself falling, and then an excruciating pain as the back of his head smashed onto a rock. He heard a sharp ringing in his ears and everything went black.

Daniel lay on something damp and smooth. He grabbed a handful and held it above his face. Wet silt! Some peculiar things circled high in the air above him like giant pelicans. Slowly, he eased himself up on his elbow, conscious of his throbbing head. He was on a muddy beach of some sort, right next to a large body of water that stretched as far as he could see. Reeds in the shallows swayed gently in the warm breeze. That's when he noticed large indentations scattered all over the mud at the water's edge. He sat up and gasped. Giant footprints! And he was lying in one!

Behind him, a dense wooded area echoed with odd screeching sounds. Although it looked like a normal forest at first glance, when he studied it, he recognized pines, yews, and magnolia trees with huge blossoms. There also seemed to be sycamores and ferns, and some kind of berry bushes.

At the edge of the shore, what looked like a *Cimolopteryx* preened itself. A prehistoric shorebird – how could that be? The knock on the head must have altered his thoughts somehow. Maybe he was unconscious and dreaming?

Daniel closed his eyes and took a deep breath. Cautiously, he opened them again, but the view hadn't changed. A loud screech came from directly overhead. He became aware of his heart thumping loudly in his chest like the steady beat of the drum in a marching band.

Gently he touched the sore spot on the back of his head and felt something sticky. When he looked at his fingers, he found blood. This was too real! Daniel willed himself to wake up. He pinched his arms and legs. Nothing changed. He was still on the muddy beach, amid numerous large, weirdly shaped footprints.

He heard a droning sound, growing louder, and a giant dragonfly drifted into view. Its iridescent yellowish wings spanned over half a metre, sprouting from a brilliant blue abdomen attached to a bright green thorax. It hovered for a few seconds, staring at him with beady dark eyes, then disappeared into the trees. Daniel gaped in disbelief.

Moments later, Daniel noticed subtle rustling movements approaching him. A small mammal, like nothing he'd ever seen before, emerged from the underbrush and sniffed the air in his direction. His wound! He had to wash away the blood and stop the flow so it wouldn't attract predators. Regardless of where he was, he was sure animals were all the same and that some species could smell fresh blood from a long distance away. Already he'd begun to attract attention.

He climbed out of the huge three-toed footprint and

slid over to the water's edge, carefully easing his backpack onto the ground. Keeping a sharp lookout, he rummaged around until he found his *Receptaculites* fossil wrapped in an old cloth. He carried his special find with him everywhere.

The "taculite," as he called it, had criss-cross markings on it like a ripe sunflower or a plastic netted bag around onions in the grocery store. This "sunflower coral" dated from 450 million years earlier. Daniel carefully removed the fossil and slipped it into his pocket. Then he dunked the cloth in water, and washed his wound with trembling fingers.

By the time he was finished, his dark hair was washed clear of blood. He held the cloth tightly over the gash at the back of his head, and replaced his backpack. He had been joined on the shore by a large turtle with a metre-long reddish brown shell and dark green paddle-like feet. Small, greenish grey, fast-moving lizards scurried across the wet ground, chasing peculiar-looking insects.

Where was he? And why couldn't he wake up or shake these weird illusions? If he didn't know better, he'd think he was in some sort of prehistoric time. Suddenly, realization dawned on him. What if he really had flipped into another time?

Instinctively, he knew that somehow he'd entered prehistoric time and he was in grave danger. This was no dream. Nor was it his wild imaginings. He wasn't sure about what time period he was in or what kind of danger he was facing. But he knew he had to hide quickly before something noticed him as easy prey out in the open. Then somehow he had to find a way home.

Keeping watch for anything that moved in his direction, he crab-walked stealthily towards the trees and several large clumps of tall, fernlike plants called cycads. He made awkward progress, propelling himself with one hand, while he pressed the cloth to his head to prevent further bleeding. He avoided strange-looking insects, flicking them away with small sticks or a thrust of his foot. Oversized butterflies and peculiar bees flitted among the colourful flowers carpeting the ground on the edge of the forest.

CRACK!! CRACK!!

A series of huge splintering sounds sent him dashing headlong into the nearest clump of fern. He rolled himself into a ball and shook for a few moments as he tried to regain his regular breathing pattern. He heard little squawking noises nearby. Peering about in the expansive fronds, he wondered what else was in there with him. Then he spotted a nest with eggs twice the size of goose eggs and two very new slimy green hatchlings of some sort, struggling for their voices. Yikes! Good thing the mother wasn't home. He had to get out of here!

Down on his knees, he peered cautiously out of the fern, but ducked back in at the sound of another crash of branches breaking and the loud cracking of something moving his way. An *Edmontosaurus* clumped through the trees, tall as an elephant, seeming to be in a hurry. Several small cat-sized animals scurried into the foliage, instantly skirting Daniel in surprise when they saw him.

Moments after the *Edmontosaurus* passed by, there were loud thumping and crunching sounds, then a vicious snapping. The ground shook with giant tremors and a *Tyrannosaurus rex* lumbered into view. Daniel cowered and made himself as small as he could as it approached. By the time the giant lizard reached him, all he could see were its heavily muscled legs and the broad-based scaly tail. If Daniel stood up, he'd only come halfway to its knees.

As the massive head with vicious yellow eyes and huge serrated teeth scoured the area, Daniel shrunk tighter against the innermost base of the fern. He held his breath until he thought he'd burst. The *T. rex* seemed to hang around forever. Its huge head nosed at a patch of ferns as it cleared a path, searching for its next meal. Daniel hoped it wasn't going to be him! If the *T. rex* grabbed him in its jaws, one crunching snap and he'd be gone. He prayed it couldn't smell his blood. *T. rexes* were known to be carrion eaters, and although Daniel wasn't dead yet, the fresh blood might be all this one needed to trigger its hunger.

Another booming crash sounded to the right. The *Tyrannosaurus rex* raised its scaled head and sniffed in a loud, snorting breath. Its eyes bulged and widened in fierce anticipation. Suddenly, it let out a thundering roar, as if warning off competitors.

THWACK!!! Its huge tale swung past Daniel's hiding place and crunched into some small trees as it headed after the *Edmontosaurus.* Huge clawed back feet crushed everything underneath as it moved along on its muscular tree stumplike back legs. The ground trembled. As it passed, Daniel looked up and saw an old healed scar along its leathery back. Maybe it was from a claw wound during a fight?

The *T. rex* left small trees uprooted and large patches of ground disturbed where its claws penetrated the earth. Small mammals followed in its wake, snatching at tiny insectlike creatures that lay injured or dead on the ground along a wide swath cut by the clawed feet and flicking tail of the hungry *T. rex.*

There was no time to lose. Daniel had to find a safe hiding place. He could hear the squawking in the nest beside him intensify and the mother was surely nearby. He wasn't going to wait around to find out what kind of dinosaur or other reptile would make a meal of him. But where could he go? And which way was safe?

Just then something large plunged towards the bracken and into the nest beside him, protesting loudly. Daniel leaped out of the fern. Running in a crouched position, he scoured the skies and the ground, hoping that nothing saw him as he headed for a clump of small bushes. Back towards the beach, he saw several long-necked thescelosaurs, turning away from the water. At the horrific sounds of the *T. rex,* they lifted their heads and bleated a shrill, eerie warning that echoed throughout the forest. Then they disappeared into the trees.

With caution, yet as fast as he dared, Daniel separated the branches and peered inside the bushes. Then, sure nothing was nesting or living there for the moment, he crept inside, as close to the centre as he could go, and sat on the ground. He took big gulps of air to quiet the thumping in his chest. He'd never been so scared in all his life! His whole body shook. Seeing a *T. rex* skeleton was one thing, but seeing a live one in the gruesome, grey, knobbly flesh was horrifying!

He thought then about "Scotty," the skeleton of a *T. rex* found near Eastend. He'd seen the dig where it'd been retrieved. Could he have just seen Scotty in the flesh? How could he tell? There didn't seem to be any way of distinguishing them. All he knew was that they were dreadful in real life!

When his hands quit shaking, he removed the cloth from his head and checked his wound. Good, it had stopped bleeding. Quietly, he unzipped his backpack and pulled a bottle of water out. He rinsed the rag, and tied it around his head tightly so that the cut wasn't exposed and wouldn't bleed again. Then he took a good long drink of the refreshing water. Abruptly he stopped drinking. How long was the water going to have to last? Worried now, he screwed the lid on tight and tucked the bottle away.

As he bent to check the contents of his backpack, a giant scorpion appeared on the ground beside him. He jumped aside and kicked it away with his foot. He scoured the area quickly, and then settled down again, looking nervously about the underbrush.

Good thing he'd brought plenty of water and food. Originally he'd expected to spend the day at his hideout, sorting through his belongings and checking for other fossils. With that in mind, his mother had helped him prepare lunch, making sure he had three bottles of water and a couple of ham-and-cheese sandwiches. How long would he be holed up in these scratchy ferns? How long would the food have to last?

Luckily, he'd also thrown in a bag of potato chips and some granola bars, besides his regular stash of chocolate bars, and some beef jerky for Dactyl. Mrs. Lindstrom, his best friend Jed's mom, had tucked in a huge piece of her special chocolate zucchini cake. She had dropped in for morning coffee to discuss the menus for the summer tourists, and brought a sample of her latest recipe experiment. He thought of it hungrily, but decided not to attract any more attention to himself until he got his bearings in this strange world of freaky sounds and unusual animals.

He pawed through his backpack to refresh his memory of other things he'd brought that might prove to be useful. Mentally he checked off the items: a freshly recharged flashlight – good for nighttime, if he had to stay that long. The matches were only good if he felt safe enough to use them without danger of attracting some prehistoric beast. Or maybe he could use a fire to scare them away! The dinosaur handbook would come in handy for identification, if he had time to do any research. His hooded fleece jacket was a definite bonus, but he wasn't sure how useful his compass would be, because he didn't have a clue which direction was home. And, since there didn't seem to be any rocks, his rock hammer wouldn't be useful in the normal way. These things were all he had to survive with. His other gear was at the hideout. Wherever that might be now!

Back in his own time, his secret cave was only a few hundred yards and several hills away from Ole Pederson's property, where Roxanne, the almost complete *Edmontosaurus* skeleton, with a fossilized nest of eggs, had been found. This special find had resulted in a small paleontological museum being set up in their hometown of Climax, with Pederson as the chief curator and local expert. The dinosaur dig operation had grown out of that as a way for Daniel's family to keep their farm viable. Daniel had never been more thrilled in his life.

A small rustling nearby quieted these happy thoughts, reminding him of his predicament. What was out there now? He tried to recall all the creatures associated with the later Cretaceous Period, for that was the time he'd identified by the flowering trees, insects, and other creatures he'd seen. He was reasonably sure he had to have travelled back about 65 to 67 million years, as the megavertebrates like the *T. rex* and *Triceratops* were only known to exist then. And even if most of his memory hadn't shut down in shock, no one knew for sure which ones were dangerous to humans. He'd just assume they all were and avoid them as best he could while he figured out how to get home. Being alone without another human being, listening to the eerily strange sounds echoing through the dense, marshy forest, spooked him.

Even worse was the fact that no one was expecting him back until later in the evening. He was known for being gone for hours. They wouldn't even come looking for him until after dark. And when they did, how could they figure out what had happened to him? Daniel shuddered.

CHAPTER TWO

Daniel sat silently contemplating his terrifying dilemma. How long could he stay here? And just where was here? He sure wished Dactyl were with him. He wouldn't feel so alone. No! On second thought, he didn't wish that for a moment. Dactyl might have become some dinosaur's dinner by now.

From the distance, a terrible roar and then some agonized bellowing rent the air, followed by loud crashing and something that sounded like trees being wrenched from the ground. The *T. rex* must have caught the *Edmontosaurus*! Or maybe something was attacking the *T. rex*, like a herd of *Triceratops* or some kind of raptors. Daniel cowered tightly into his hiding place, as the whole forest became alive with a cacophony of loud, terrifying sounds. What was he going to do? He couldn't sit here, waiting forever. How was he going to get back home? And where was a safe place to go in the meantime?

He peeked through the bushes. Maybe he should

make a move while all the creatures were focused on the *T. rex* battle? He knew the vast, never-ending sea trapped him from behind. And the horrific battle sounds seemed to be coming from his left, so that meant he'd have to go straight ahead or right, into the trees. Straight ahead was still too close to the fight and that was the direction the *T. rex* had come from in the beginning. So, right it was!

This seemed a good choice as the trees were growing on a slight rise. If only he could reach some higher ground, he might be able to get his bearings. Daniel moved quickly, yet stealthily, so as not to scare anything or attract attention to himself. All of his muscles tensed at the pressure of not knowing what he'd find or how quickly he'd have to react. His stomach did flip-flops and his head ached with each step he took; still, he didn't dare stop to rest.

At first he followed a bit of a path that led away from the sea through the forest. But what if he met something fearsome and huge coming for a drink? He decided to choose routes that seemed less travelled, yet where he didn't need to create a new path through the plant growth, for fear the sounds he made would draw attention to his movements.

The air was humid and full of strange piercing sounds. Every once in a while he heard little rustlings in the spongy undergrowth and odd plops, as if something had cascaded to the forest floor. Tiny plants and flowers poked through the decay of fallen leaves and twigs beneath his feet with each bouncy step he took. He rocked over slippery hidden roots and tangled vines. He'd seen similar vegetation on the hike he'd taken with his parents in the La Ronge forest area a few years before when they were visiting relatives. Then he'd been warned of bears and had even seen claw marks on the trees. That was a piece of cake compared to what he might find now!

Sometimes huge broken stumps and decaying fallen logs lying at odd angles blocked Daniel's path. Cautiously, he made his way through dense stands of cycads and sycamore, noticing four-metre spikes of horsetail shooting up erratically. He knew it was one of the few prehistoric plants that still existed in the current world, although they were only a few centimetres high now, and probably a relative rather than a direct descendant of the original ones.

In places dead trees stood, waiting for a strong wind to topple them over, many covered with wide streamers of lichen, giving a ghostly feeling in the darkening forest. Small meadows appeared less frequently, and the gashes in trees were deeper and far longer and higher than anything he'd ever seen before. Occasional whistling calls ricocheted through the treetops.

Every once in a while, small mammals scurried across his path. He stopped in his tracks and waited for everything to be still and quiet again before venturing forward. Mostly he ignored the butterflies and moths, but kept a wary eye for bees and the possibility of spiders. He didn't even want to think about poisonous snakes!

After several more minutes of following a bend in the path, he saw large marshy areas speckled with rushes and floating yellow flowers. He bent to take a closer look at the water lilies, and then stepped around a particularly large tree. Suddenly, an opossum-like mammal darted into his path. Startled, they both stared at one another for a split second, before the unsuspecting creature gave a long piercing shriek that echoed through the forest and then bounded away. It seemed to be hunting insects.

Daniel gasped and leaned against the tree trunk, his legs feeling abruptly weak. This was almost more than he could take! He waited for a reaction to the call, but nothing else rushed out at him. His stomach gurgled with hunger. Softly, he retrieved a water bottle and took a long swig. But he was afraid to remove any of the food, in case the noise and smells brought danger his way. He'd better find a place to hide soon. The pale sun was beginning to sink down to the treetops, casting an eerie glow over the landscape. If only he could find a safe place to rest before nightfall.

As if in sudden answer to his prayers, when he rounded the next curve, he saw a clearing and, a few yards in the distance, a forest of towering trees. They looked like the giant redwoods he'd seen in photos of the forest in California. If he could reach them and climb one of them, he might be able to see a panoramic view of the scene below. He scanned the area quickly and determined the best way to proceed.

The day's last piercing rays of sun warmed his back, and the undergrowth was dense and slippery from the moist air. Sometimes his feet slid off the mossy path, leaving him mired in weedy muck. Small rivulets of sweat trickled down his face from the humidity. His body felt clammy and his hands sticky, making progress slow. Besides this, his head throbbed from the original accident when he hit his head.

He sure wished he were home in bed with his mom taking care of him. Being a nurse, she'd know just what to do and what medicine to prescribe to make the pain go away. Right now, it was all he could do to keep his footing and move onwards without succumbing to certain death all around him. Soupy swamp and wet patches of grassy hummocks made walking difficult.

By the time he reached the edge of the redwoods, Daniel's legs were scraped and his runner-clad feet sore and soaking wet. He was too weak to go any further. When he spied a huge hollow tree trunk that seemed unoccupied, with a small opening in front, he made his way over to it. The space was just big enough for him to sit inside. Little pellets like mouse droppings, bits of branches, and dead leaves were strewn on the musty dirt floor, which angled upwards slightly from the opening.

As he peered about, he realized that all he could see was more swampy forest. Along the way, he hadn't seen any well-known predators, but then he wasn't thinking straight and couldn't recall which of the Cretaceous creatures might search for food where he sat. He hoped this would be a safe place to stay, at least for a bit.

No longer able to ignore his hunger, he slowly unzipped his backpack and slipped out a sandwich, furtively watching the scene around him. From this particular spot, he couldn't see much below, but maybe that meant nothing could see him either! Chomping his sandwich quickly, and washing it down his dry throat with big gulps of water, Daniel soon finished the first one. He was just about to reach for another, when he thought again about how long he might have to stay in the prehistoric world. His other sandwich might have to last a long time!

Suddenly, he felt drained and tired. He stretched his body out as best he could in the cramped tree stump on the uneven, slanted ground. Using the backpack for a pillow, he tried to rest. He felt like a cat with one eye open for danger, and found little relief at first, jumping at every unusual sound. He was afraid of rolling out of his hiding spot if he made an unconscious move. His eyelids felt heavy, and he knew if he gave way to the drowsiness, he'd fall asleep. Aside from the unknown dangers around him, he also was afraid to doze off for fear his head might be concussed enough to keep him from waking up quickly.

As he struggled with exhaustion, a sudden scratching sound brought him abruptly upright. Something was above him in a crevice of the tree! He held his breath and waited. More scraping. Then silence.

Warily, he stood up and scanned the hollow space above him in the heavy gloom. At first he couldn't make out any shapes, but then he noticed an almost oval opening several yards above. Lightning must have split the trunk at one time, and a heavy, misshapen branch protruded from the fracture. He realized that some sort of huge twiggy nest sat perched partly in the opening and partly in the crevice of the branch.

No more sounds came for a few moments. He took a deep breath, braced his feet against the inner walls of the tree trunk, and climbed upwards as if he were scaling a rock chimney. Just as he poked his head above the mound through the opening, another scuffling sound erupted.

Daniel jerked back and nearly fell, but not before he'd seen the inside of the giant nest! The walls were about thirty centimetres high and made from a mixture of twigs, lichen, and some kind of matted seaweed. Several huge eggs, one with a slightly cracked shell, were huddled in the middle of the forty-five-centimetre circumference. As he watched, a gangly, sharp-beaked, wet creature emerged from the cracked egg.

Drawing back watchfully, Daniel contemplated his latest find. He wanted another look at the nest. He moved as quietly as he could, keeping a vigilant eye on the peach-hued skies for the return of the parents. Obviously, they must be some kind of flying reptile, but what? And were the creatures dangerous?

As he drew himself up for another look at the nest,

Daniel found himself thinking about the climate. Were there seasons here like back home? Was it spring, when baby birds hatched and other animals had their offspring? He certainly had seen a great many nests along the way. He knew some scientists figured there were two climates in prehistoric times: wet and dry. This must be the wet one, he thought, wiping the moisture off his forehead.

Then another thought struck him. There was no way he was high enough to escape predators. He needed to be way up in the tree. The trick was how to get there. From inside the tree trunk, he could go as far as the nest, but after that he'd have to scale the outside of the tree.

Daniel dropped back to the ground, took a drink of water, and pulled on his backpack. Nervously, he wiped his hands on his jeans to dry them off. Then, taking a deep breath, he began scaling the interior of the trunk again. He did another awkward crablike climb, lodging his feet wherever he could, and bracing his back against the inner tree as he pulled himself up with his hands. Warily, he stayed on the lookout for danger above and below as he scaled upwards.

When he reached the nest, the squawking of the one hatched creature increased. So did the sweat pouring off Daniel's forehead. He wiped his face with his hand and contemplated how to climb around the nest, quickly. He sure didn't want to tip it – or worse, end up in it! Nor did he want to be something's dinner!

He managed to squeeze himself through the narrow

opening between the branch and the nest, feeling the bark scrape along his back and arms. Carefully, he swung himself onto the branch and stood there catching his breath. The squawking coming from the nest increased as another gangly creature hatched. He had to get a move on!

As he eased himself partway around the tree trunk, he stretched for another large branch, barely within reach. He managed to pull himself over to it. For a few moments, he dangled precariously until his feet found a ridge in the bark of the trunk to rest on.

Momentarily, fear immobilized Daniel. He didn't dare look down! But the fear of being torn apart by the sabre-sharp teeth of a *Tyrannosaurus rex* spurred him on. He eased his body closer to the trunk of the tree, keeping an arm around the bough. Holding tight, he pulled himself up into a sitting position on the branch. His head pounded and his chest heaved. He leaned against the sturdy trunk and went limp, breathing hard. He closed his eyes and rested for several minutes.

When he opened them, he found himself overlooking the ghostly expanse of the forest in the fading light. Beyond was the vast sea, peppered with small, marshy islands. The mouth of a river stemmed from the forest, from the direction the *T. rex* had come earlier, flowing into the sea. Around him, a hubbub of noise louder than anything he was used to in his everyday life: weird bird calls, insects keening, splashes of something sloshing through the marshes, a slight breeze, crunching of undergrowth in the trees, branches snapping.

As Daniel speculated about his environment, he scoured the scene below. There seemed to be no sign of the *T. rex*. Through the darkening forest, he could just make out a ravaged area in the distance with uprooted trees and a large carcass of some kind – maybe the *Edmontosaurus*. Small animals ripped at its flesh, and huge pterosaur-like winged creatures flew overhead. One at a time they swooped down and plucked at the carcass, tearing off remnants. Fascinated, Daniel watched until one of them swung towards his hiding place. He scrunched himself against the tree trunk, trying not to let his movements show. He figured these prehistoric buzzards probably had great eyesight!

Moments later, he heard the great whoosh of air as the pterosaur flapped closer and a jostling of twigs signalled its landing on the nest. A terrible stench, like rotting meat, surged Daniel's way. He couldn't tell if it was the smell of carrion or the pterosaur that made him gag. He held his hand over his nose and breathed as noiselessly as possible through his mouth, listening to the mother's strange shrieking, as irritating as nails scraping down a blackboard at school. He imagined her examining the eggs on the branch below him. Little crackling sounds came next. Then he heard a small chirruplike screech similar to an old unoiled door hinge. Another baby had hatched!

The mother remained for several more minutes, although it seemed like hours to Daniel. His eyes watered from the reek of strong, unfamiliar smells. Just when he didn't think he could stand it anymore, she lifted off, circled the tree, and headed back down to the feasting site. As she did so, Daniel mentally compared her size and wingspan to the diagrams in his books and figured she must be a *Pteranodon.*

Nightfall covered the forest, and Daniel could barely see any movement below. Once he saw a thirty-foot *Triceratops* with its expansive bony frill protruding off its shoulders, two long horns above its eyes, and the shorter horn above its parrotlike beak. A small herd of some kind of night-feeder, no bigger than a white-tailed deer, but lizardlike, with sharp claws on short forearms and longish whipping tails, feasted on insects for a while, then disappeared into the dark. Everything seemed to go silent at once, and then he could only hear the odd nocturnal sound. The twilight faded quickly from the skies, but Daniel knew he couldn't stay where he was for the night, breathing in the horrible stink when the mother returned.

With the little light left, he sidled his way off the branch and descended partway down to the next branch. As he reached what he thought was solid footing, he slipped. Although he managed to grab a good hold of a protruding limb above and eventually righted himself, he sent a multitude of bark pieces and twigs tumbling below. They clattered into the nighttime stillness, echoing deafeningly like the demolition of a high-rise brick building. Daniel cringed, waiting for the sounds to die away.

Suddenly, he heard quick, pulsating whooshes. The

mother *Pteranodon* was just above him. Daniel held his breath and closed his eyes tight, tensing his muscles and willing the creature to leave. He clutched the side of the rough trunk, pressing himself against it, trying to blend in. His knuckles went numb. His toes cramped from the tight curl he had them in as he desperately tried not to move and at the same time to keep his sneakers from slipping again. He held his muscles so tight, they hurt. Great drafts of air made by the pterosaur whistled in his ears, and he shivered with the coolness.

When the gust of wind subsided, Daniel opened his eyes slightly. The huge winged reptile circled above, then swooped back down, heading directly towards him. He was too exposed! Quickly, he searched for a way down or a better branch to hide in. If he could just make the limb to his left, he could scramble into a tight crevice. Although her beak was long and narrow, maybe the *Pteranodon* couldn't reach him. He saw the massive dark creature looming closer with every giant wing flap. He had to take a chance.

Daniel leapt! But he'd left it too long. The force of the gust of air from the downward draft of the wing flap sent him off-kilter. Tiny twigs, cones, and branches fell from above, hitting him. He grasped at a small limb. But the tip of a huge featherless wing caught him across the back, giving him a horrific thump that sent him crashing front-first against the tree trunk. He heard a cracking sound, just before everything went black!

CHAPTER THREE

Daniel couldn't breathe! With the wind knocked out of him, he lay on the ground paralyzed with fear, willing his body and his lungs to work. Several agonizing seconds passed. Then at last he was able to take in a huge gush of air. Sharp pains seared his lungs as he gasped to regain his regular breathing pattern. Even without moving, he felt every part of his body aching, inside and out.

Slowly, he opened his eyes to see a bright summer sun in a clear blue sky. With his hands at his sides, he clutched at the ground beneath him. Clumps of grass! He was home! Or at least he wasn't in dinosaur time, anyway, because he knew that grasses hadn't evolved until later in the Tertiary Period. How long had he been gone?

He raised his head and, several yards away, saw the large pile of rocks where the Nelwins had ambushed him. In the distance, he saw the figures of Craig and Todd hurrying across the familiar undulating hills. Had they tried to move him? Were they going for help? Or were they just leaving him here?

Daniel groaned. He had no strength to call after them. He'd best not wait for their return. He lay anxiously in pain, not sure how to move first. He'd just lived through the most terrifying incident in his life and his whole body felt limp, like his Aunt Deb's overcooked spaghetti. He shivered. Well, he couldn't stay where he was much longer.

Easing himself into a sitting position, he examined the back of his head. Gingerly, he pulled the rag away, grimacing as it stuck to the crust of the wound. As he unwound the cloth, something dribbled into his eyes. He brushed at it with his fingers, feeling scratches on his forehead and more blood. He must have cut himself when he smashed headfirst into the side of the tree after the *Pteranodon*'s wing clipped him. What a close call!

But how had he ever gone back into prehistoric time? As he thought about his situation, pangs of hunger jabbed his stomach. He hungrily opened his backpack, ate another sandwich, the bag of chips, and the piece of cake, washing it all down with big gulps of water. Revived somewhat, he decided to head for home to clean up. He also had to find his dog.

"Dactyl, here, boy!" Daniel shouted feebly, but the words didn't have much volume behind them. "Dactyl!" he called again.

He didn't have the strength to call any louder, so he started for home without his pet, knowing he'd eventually show up. But it wasn't until he reached the flat part of the pasture leading to the farmyard that Dactyl came scampering up to him. When Daniel bent to pet him, the dog sniffed, and whined, and sniffed some more. Then he gave a snuffling sneeze and ran ahead.

"Thanks a lot, pal!" Daniel called after his retreating pet. "You'd smell bad too, if you'd been where I was."

When Daniel finally arrived in the yard, he found his mom in the garden weeding with Cheryl. His two-year-old sister chortled in delight when she saw him, running to him on chubby little legs. Mom wasn't quite as pleased to see his condition.

"What on earth happened to you?" She demanded, dropping her hoe in the row of string beans and hurrying over to examine his wounds. "You've been gone less than a half-hour and look at the mess you're in." Her brown eyes widened in concern.

She picked up Cheryl and marched Daniel into the house. He didn't mind the fuss his mom made over him. He was just glad to be home.

Mom directed him to a chair at the kitchen table and quickly filled a basin with warm water. She dabbed at his wound with a warm washcloth, removing the grit and flaking dried blood.

"Let's just say I had a little run-in with a few rocks," Daniel explained when Mom pressed him for an answer.

"What were you doing?" She examined the dirt and the rips in his T-shirt.

"Climbing. Maybe where I shouldn't have been," he answered, not sure how to explain where he'd really been. The thought of the attacking *Pteranodon* made him shiver.

"It looks like a little more than that," Mom said, dabbing at his wounds with iodine.

"Ouch!" he complained. "Take it easy."

"Let's hear the whole story, then," she said with concern, pushing a straggle of blonde hair that had escaped from her ponytail out of her eyes.

"Oh, all right! It was those Nelwins again!" he admitted. "They tripped me and I landed on some rocks. No big deal, Mom."

"No big deal! Look at you, and your torn clothes!" Her face got that angry, determined look Daniel didn't like, because it usually meant trouble for whoever crossed her.

"First I'm taking you to the hospital to have you checked for concussion, and then I'm going to march over there and speak to their father about this."

"No, Mom, don't. You know that'll only make it worse. Their dad will only get mean to them, and they'll get meaner to me. And I don't need to go to the hospital!"

She checked Daniel's eyes carefully, lifting his lids and moving her fingers in front of them to make sure he was tracking properly.

"Fine, I'll talk this over with your dad when he gets home," Mom said, efficiently bandaging his cuts. Then she gave him some Tylenol and told him to lie down for a while until it kicked in.

"I don't want you to go out there again today," she said, scooping up Cheryl and heading back outside.

"Aw, Mom, they're gone now. There won't be any more trouble."

"Well, maybe not, but I'd rather you stuck around here." She anxiously scanned him from top to bottom.

Daniel gave her a withering look. She stopped short and smiled at him.

"Oh, all right. I guess there's no sense in punishing you for something they did wrong. Go ahead when you're feeling better. But be careful to stay out of their way."

"You bet I will," answered Daniel. Then to himself he added, "Easier said than done with those two wily guys!"

Wrinkling her nose, she added, "You could use a bath and some clean clothes, too." With that she carried Cheryl out the door.

Daniel rested on the couch, where he watched the last few minutes of a cartoon show. His eyelids felt heavy. He vaguely recalled his mother tiptoeing in to check on him at one point. He awoke fully an hour and a half later to the sounds of his family coming in for lunch.

Scrambling upstairs for a quick shower, he then joined them at the kitchen table for another "snack." Dealing with dinosaurs had made him hungry.

Dad did a double take when he stepped into the kitchen and saw Daniel's bandaged head.

"Now what?" he asked, shaking his head in disbelief.

"The Nelwins," Mom responded before Daniel could

open his mouth. She gave Cheryl some homemade macaroni and cheese and passed the bowl to Dad. Then she set the salad on the table and served everyone a hot dog.

Dad's face tightened. "Something has to be done about those boys! Their dad sure isn't going to do anything to straighten them out. He'd never stay sober long enough, even if he did consider disciplining them. Maybe it's time to bring in the law?"

By the concentrated look on Mom's face, she seemed to be agreeing quite seriously with him. For her petite size, she could be feisty and determined when she needed to be.

"Not yet, Dad," Daniel protested. "It'll be my word against theirs and there are two of them. I won't be able to prove anything. Besides, that'll only make things worse for me."

"Not if they're locked up for a while!" Dad responded briskly, dishing some macaroni onto Daniel's plate, then serving himself.

Daniel shifted nervously in his chair as he picked at his food. "They wouldn't be there for long. Their dad would have them out in no time."

Although he didn't take much notice of his sons, Horace Nelwin wouldn't like them spending any time in the slammer. He'd bully everyone involved until they let them loose. Daniel wouldn't be safe for long, if they were even locked up at all.

"Even a few hours might give them time to think about their actions and the consequences," Dad added.

"At least we'd have a little peace for a few months," said Mom. Her brown eyes had gone dark and determined.

"But that'll only give them time to think of worse things to do to me! How about we hold on a bit?" Daniel objected. "First, let me figure out a way to stop them."

Mom opposed the idea instantly. "Daniel, you could get seriously hurt. Look at you now."

He was sure he looked quite the ghastly sight with bandages on his head and scratches on his arms. They couldn't even see the ones on his legs. Daniel bit his lip to keep from blurting out his adventure in the prehistoric world. The Nelwins were nothing compared to the *T. rex* and the *Pteranodon* he'd encountered, but he couldn't tell his parents about that! Besides, he wasn't even sure if it was real.

"I don't think they meant for me to be hurt. They were probably just trying to follow me and find my hideout," he said, shovelling some macaroni into his mouth and chewing quickly.

"Great, now they're stalking you!" Mom said in exasperation.

"I'll just keep a closer eye out for them and stay out of their way," Daniel declared, reaching for the mustard and smearing it on his hot dog. "They won't be back today, and I won't have another chance to go to the hideout for awhile." Then he added hopefully, "Maybe the problem will just go away."

Dad rolled his eyes. Mom shook her head, but her mouth was tight in disapproval. Dad glowered at a spot behind Daniel's head, calming himself down before he spoke again.

"I'll be back in time for supper and chores," Daniel said, rising from the table with his hot dog in his hand.

"Just a minute, young man." Mom rose from the table, checked his bandages and his eyes again, and then looked questioningly at Dad.

Dad shrugged his shoulders. Mom sighed. Daniel grabbed his backpack, and shoved more refilled bottles of water into it. He still had his other snacks, and he didn't think he'd be hungry again for quite some time. He gave Cheryl a quick tickle and a hug, and then headed towards the door. As he bent to tie his runners, Mom came over and slipped a baggy of fresh oatmeal raisin cookies into his hand. They smiled at one another, and without a word, Daniel left.

Even before the door closed, he could hear his parents discussing the Nelwins again. He thought he heard Dad say something about "Maybe the boy has to learn to fight his own battles,'" and Mom protesting. Then Dad said, "We'll step in when we have to."

He stopped to listen more when he heard Dad say, "They're no different than Horace was when he was a boy. I know. I grew up with him."

Then Mom said, "I feel sorry for them, being brought up without a mother and not always having enough to eat, but that's no excuse for bullying people!"

"You're right, of course. It's just too bad they didn't have a better role model than their father, or at least some purpose or interest in their lives instead of hurting others."

Daniel heard the scrape of the chair as his father left the table, and he tiptoed out the door and headed towards his hideout. The afternoon sun was high in the blue sky, with large puffy clouds that looked like they were in a painting, but there wasn't a bit of a breeze and the air felt muggy as he headed through the pasture gate.

The Nelwins really were a problem, but for the moment he didn't see how to deal with those two bullies. They'd been that way for as long as Daniel had known them. Right now, he was more interested in getting to his hideout and checking out his stash of fossils. He thought about how he'd come to be in the world of dinosaurs and back again. Probably the knock on his head had caused a hallucination!

He chose a different way to go this time, totally avoiding the heap of rocks and the coulee of trees where the Nelwins had hidden. From now on, he'd stay well in the open so he could see long distances. No one was going to ambush him again. He also kept Dactyl occupied and closer to his side, playing fetch with the stick, instead of letting him dash off to chase gophers and rabbits.

Once he neared his hideout, Daniel looked at it from a different perspective – that of someone trying to locate the place. The first thing he noticed was the clanging of tin cans and bones tied to a piece of twine that warned him of intruders when he was inside his cave. He could hear it from some distance off, and that meant others could too. It wouldn't be long before someone found his hideout by the sounds alone. Even his best friend, Jed, who was always getting lost! He smiled to himself, remembering a couple of incidents last summer where Jed had headed across a field in the wrong direction to deliver lunch to his father and ended up at a neighbour's house.

A year and a half ago, Daniel had been worried about intrusions from Pederson. Then they'd discovered their common interest in dinosaurs and had become friends. Now he just had to worry about others. Which was worse? Having someone find the hideout because of the noise made by his homemade alarm, or him being startled by someone while he was inside? He removed the twine and carefully put the tin cans and bones away. If no one could find the hideout, they wouldn't intrude on him either.

The next thing he realized was that the area around the structure of the cave was too tidy and the entrance too easily observed. Although the hideout was well hidden with branches and logs covered with soil and grass, so that it looked like a natural mound between the two hills, he had cleaned the area around the opening too well. Something had to be done!

Daniel poked around with a long stick to make sure there were no rattlesnakes coiled underneath the scrub and rocks. Then he picked up branches and dragged them across the doorway and around the hideout, making everything look as natural as possible. Dactyl yanked at ends of the branches with his teeth, hoping for a game of tug-of-war. Daniel played with him a bit, but soon took his work seriously, and Dactyl wandered off without his noticing.

Some time later, Daniel surveyed the work he'd completed from a certain distance away. Satisfied that he'd accomplished his objective, which was that his hideout didn't stand out in any way, he returned to the entrance and crawled inside. Dactyl appeared suddenly and pushed his way in beside him, knocking down some of the branches. Daniel did a little repair work, then pulled over his tree-stump stool and relaxed under the ceiling opening, through which the mid-afternoon sun streamed in ribbons across the cavern walls.

He opened his backpack and pulled out some beef jerky for Dactyl, then poured him some water in an old metal pot. He took a drink from the water bottle while he surveyed the contents of his hideout: plastic ice cream pails of rocks and fossils, a tattered research book on dinosaurs, deer antlers, a special rattlesnake skin, an old sleeping bag, his excavation tools, and his emergency stash of snacks, candles, and matches.

Emptying his backpack onto the packed dirt floor of the cave, he sorted through his things and put them away into their appropriate containers. Besides the bottles of water, which he stashed near the back of the cavern to keep cool, only two things remained on the ground at the end. One was his *Receptaculites* fossil that he always took with him. The other was a piece of bark he'd never seen before. Where had it come from? He couldn't remember collecting it. Puzzled, Daniel bent to retrieve it when he heard a shrill, birdlike whistle.

Pederson! That was their secret code. Daniel hustled over to the doorway and gave a return whistle. Dactyl bulldozed his way past Daniel again and ran excitedly to join Pederson and his dog, Bear. Daniel crawled out and joined the others partway up the hillside.

"Looks like you've been un-improving the place, Daniel Bringham," Pederson called out as he approached, his eyes twinkling in amusement. Then he noticed the cuts. "With your face, by the looks of it."

"This happened while I was trying to keep those Nelwins away," he said, pointing to the bandaged back of his head.

Pederson's face went hard. "Those good-for-nothing louts. Someone needs to teach them a lesson or two!" He gave Bear a nod and the two dogs yipped and chased one another, then dashed off to explore together.

Daniel sighed. "Yeah, I know. I just have to figure out how."

"I'm sure you'll think of something. You have a good head on your shoulders, Daniel." Pederson patted him on the shoulder and winked at him.

Should he tell Pederson about his other adventure? He might not think Daniel was so smart then. He'd probably just figure that the knock on his head had caused some wild imaginings. Daniel himself was having a hard time believing it was anything but a delusion. But how could the extra scratches on his face be explained? And what about the fact that he'd only had one sandwich left when he came to, and the rag from around his fossil, which had been inside his backpack, had been wrapped around his head? Maybe he'd wait and think about it for a bit more before saying anything to Pederson.

"So what's up?" Daniel asked. There had to be a special reason for Pederson to come looking for him. He usually waited for Daniel to visit.

"I just got back from that town council meeting. Seems that the mayor of Climax has another brilliant idea for linking our research outpost and the town museum closer to the T.rex Discovery Centre." Pederson spoke slowly, then stopped, looking off into the distance.

Sometimes Daniel thought Pederson's slowness was done on purpose just to annoy him, but he had come to know that usually it meant Pederson was reflecting on his choice of words before speaking.

After several moments, Pederson continued. "She wants me to take her ideas to our friends at the T.rex Discovery Centre to see how feasible they are before we take them to the 'powers that be' beyond us." He paused and watched the dogs on the next hill.

Daniel stared at him. "Yeah, and?" he asked impatiently.

"Thought I might as well make a trip there tomorrow before we get started on the new dig site." Pederson spat on the ground. "And..." he took his time getting out his handkerchief to blow his nose.

This time Daniel knew he was doing it to irritate him. He waited, trying not to show his impatience.

"I wondered if you'd want to go with me to Eastend in the morning?" He waited nonchalantly for Daniel to reply.

"Sometimes you ask some dumb questions, for a paleontologist," Daniel said, grinning.

He loved going to the T.rex Discovery Centre and talking with Tim Tokaryk. He was the supervising paleontologist, who worked for the Royal Saskatchewan Museum at the research station located in the centre. He and some of the other staff had worked with them on the *Edmontosaurus* dig and Mr. Tokaryk was still involved with the preparation of the skeleton.

"What time are we leaving?" asked Daniel.

"Nine a.m. too early for you?" Pederson laughed.

"Nah, that'll give me plenty of time to do my barn chores before we go."

"Okay, see you then." Pederson turned and gave a different kind of whistle that brought Bear back to his side. He waved, and the pair headed for home.

Daniel hesitated. Maybe he should call Pederson back and tell him about his bizarre experience, after all? For an old guy, he was pretty open-minded most of the time. But maybe this time he wouldn't believe him. Daniel could barely believe what had happened himself. No, he'd wait until he'd done some research and figured a few things out first. Maybe he'd find some answers at the T.rex Discovery Centre tomorrow.

CHAPTER FOUR

Daniel hurried back to his hideout to retrieve his special fossil and his backpack. Once inside, he stared at the chunk of bark on the ground, but decided to leave it where it was until his return trip. He'd make sure that happened as soon as possible. He hadn't done all the things he'd planned to do, like rigging up some other advance warning system that only he could hear inside his hideout. And maybe even making an emergency exit.

A gentle breeze blew across the hills as Daniel headed for home. He'd be on schedule to do chores, if the position of the afternoon sun was any indication. The days were longer now, and sometimes he had trouble figuring out the time. He took a deep breath and then whistled for Dactyl, who was nowhere in sight. As he swooped down to pluck a blade of grass, he thought he saw his dog way up ahead.

Daniel chewed on the grass blade as he thought about his morning adventures. Obviously, hitting his head both times had something to do with his shifting backwards and forwards in time. Surely there was an easier way to do it – not that he wanted to do go to the Cretaceous Period again! That was too scary! And it hurt too much, as the returning headache reminded him. Good thing he didn't have many chores to do now that the family had reduced their farming operation.

When he entered the barn, the air was several degrees cooler than outside, and much darker, so he turned on an overhead string of bare light bulbs. The usual array of kittens darted around him, waiting for his special attention. He sat on a straw bale and played with them. They chased a length of twine and an old bit of leather harness that he lazily dragged around the floor of the barn. Dust motes fluttered in the air with the movement. Gypsy, his horse, whinnied from outside, and at last Daniel set the twine aside and went to do his chores.

Retrieving a pail of chop – a mixture of crushed oats and sometimes other grains – from the feed room, he headed out the back door that led to the corrals and pasture. He only had to water the two horses in the nearby pasture, and milk a couple of cows. Dad had sold most of the other cattle to pay off some of his debt and he only seeded and hayed a few acres now. The rest of the feed he bought from a neighbour. And the other cows were in the pasture for the summer.

Eventually, if the dinosaur digs worked out, the Bringhams would farm in a bigger way again. For now,

Daniel still had to do his share of the farm work, although most of his spare time was spent with Pederson at a dig, or with Dad and Mr. Lindstrom as they carved out the hiking trails and plotted the campsites.

Daniel hurried outside to the fenced pasture behind the barn and past the corrals where the cows and horses patiently waited. Gypsy snorted and shook her head at him as if to let him know he'd dallied too long. He cranked on the water hose and filled the trough. Next he opened the gate, and herded the two milk cows towards the open barn door, leading them with the pail of chop.

They plodded inside, chewing their cud and flicking their tails at the small cloud of flies and mosquitoes hovering around them. He poured the chop into the troughs in their individual stalls to keep them quiet while he milked them.

The next morning, Daniel waited for Pederson at the end of the lane. He'd slept soundly, even though he'd expected to have horrible dreams, and had trouble going to sleep at first. He must have been more tired than he'd thought. When he woke up, he hugged his pillow to his chest, so happy to find himself at home in his own bed. Then he groaned. He still had a slight headache, and his legs and arms ached from climbing the tree. His bruises had turned into large black-and-blue spots on his head and body. He looked like he'd been a punching bag at boxing practice.

As he shifted against a tree at the end of the lane, he felt his arm gingerly, and winced. Moments later, Pederson rounded the trees in his rusted 1959 Studebaker Scotsman pickup and slid smoothly to a stop with a slight squeak of rusty springs. For a brief moment, Daniel patted Dactyl, who sat with pleading eyes and whined. Daniel shook his head.

"Not this time, boy!"

Dactyl thumped his tail on the ground, but soon gave up and wandered off with a wounded look on his face. Daniel hopped into the dusty truck and promptly sneezed. Although Pederson kept the engine running well, he did little to preserve the outside or clean the interior of his aging vehicle.

Besides, with the usually dry land and gravel roads that he travelled, cleaning would be almost pointless for Pederson, who was out and about regularly, especially now that he travelled back and forth to the museum in Climax and the digs on his farmland. As a result, the dash, instrument panel, seats, and floor had a thin layer of dust over them, and the odd mosquito in evidence. Daniel flicked at a small spider dangling from the bottom of the glove compartment and settled in for the jaunt to town.

"I thought we'd go the long way. Through Climax. I haven't picked up my mail in a while," Pederson said, shifting into gear. "I forgot yesterday," he admitted sheepishly. "Besides, I wouldn't mind stopping in at the museum for a minute. We'll do a loop to Eastend and come back through Shaunavon."

Daniel nodded in agreement. He didn't often get away from the farm or get to ride in Pederson's old cream-coloured truck. And he loved going to the museum. He knew Pederson couldn't stay away either. He was probably checking to make sure the volunteer staff was on time and ready to answer questions from the visitors.

As they rattled along the dust-swirled gravel road towards Highway 32, the sun shone hot in an almost cloudless blue sky. The weather forecast on the radio predicted another scorching day. Daniel could already feel the sweat forming on his forehead and his T-shirt sticking to his back against the truck seat.

The relatively flat landscape, after the heat wave of the last several weeks, looked dowdy and brown. Even the yellow flowers of the wild sweet clover growing along the ditches seemed muted and almost blended into the dry grasses. Gophers, with their stubby tails pointing upwards like short antennas, scurried daringly across the road, darting for safety into holes hidden in the dry weeds on the other side. Calls of a yellow-throated warbler and a meadowlark punctuated the morning quiet.

All at once, an unknown vehicle came up behind them in a shower of gravel and dust. Obviously, the driver was in a hurry. Daniel quickly rolled up his window to keep from choking on the swirl of thick gravel dust that enshrouded them when the truck passed them. Pederson did the same. They watched the dusty haze linger for the next mile ahead, billowing out across the fields as it dissipated. When the dust settled, they wound their windows down again. Pederson never said a word.

Once they turned onto the highway, Daniel didn't bounce around quite so much, even though Pederson did some fancy driving to miss the patches and potholes in the road. Daniel marvelled at the craggy blue-grey hills as they dipped into the Frenchman River Valley, imagining the myriad of fossils contained just below the surface. This reminded him of his wild adventure of the day before and he wondered for about the zillionth time if he should mention it to Mr. Pederson. Something always stopped him, and it did again. He'd wait until after their visit to the T.rex Centre.

As they rounded a sharp corner, they came across Herb Milner driving the local lumberyard delivery truck. Pederson slowed as Herb geared down to make the next long incline. Daniel stared with interest at a cut in the hillside that revealed interesting protrusions that he could only imagine held rare fossils, just waiting to be discovered.

Suddenly, a dark blue Dodge truck screamed up behind them. Todd Nelwin was at the wheel. Craig hung his head out of the passenger-side window and yelled at them to get out of the way. Their radio blared some distorted, thumping country tune in the background.

Pederson's face went stony and he seemed to ignore them. Todd began honking and attempting to pass.

Purposefully, Pederson kept to the speed limit and held to the proper side of the road. Even if he'd wanted to, he had no room to move over, as the narrow highway had no real shoulder. Todd's impatience escalated. He breezed by, only to brake abruptly when an oncoming car appeared over the top of the hill.

Slamming on his brakes, Pederson allowed Todd to squeeze in between him and the back of the lumber truck. The moment the car passed on the opposite side, Todd squealed out again and tore in front of Herb Milner, then disappeared down the hill, until his truck became only a speck on the horizon.

Daniel's heart fluttered against his chest. He released his grip from the dash and relaxed his feet from pushing into the floorboards. He hadn't realized he'd braced himself so hard.

"Damn fools!" Pederson swore at them, shaking his head. "They're just the type that cause innocent people to be hurt!"

"Typical Nelwin style," Daniel said, sitting back in his seat, trying to relax again. Being anywhere around Todd made him nervous. He always seemed to be angry and tended to lash out first, before thinking. Especially in school, where his big mouth and talking back to the teachers regularly netted him detention. Craig usually ended up there too, often because his brother egged him on.

A few dips and curves later, Daniel and Pederson headed across the flat stretch of land that led into Climax.

They could see the old elevators, which were no longer used, poking above the horizon several miles away. Short green crops grew in the fields on either side, extending as far as the eye could see.

The first thing they saw on the main street of town was the Nelwins' truck parked illegally at an odd angle across two spaces in front of the post office. The pair came out with their hands empty of mail, laughing and jostling one another, and jumped into the truck. Then without looking, Todd backed around until they faced the other side of the street. He drove a few yards and screeched to a halt in front of the local café.

With a slam of the truck doors they sauntered inside, purposely knocking into a young blonde-haired girl coming out the door. Her plastic shopping bag flew out of her hand and hit the ground with a clank, scattering the contents onto the sidewalk.

"Watch it, you jerks!" she said, turning to look back at them as she retrieved her drinks and bags of chips.

"Did we upset the little girl?" Craig said with exaggerated fake anxiety, and laughing. The pair guffawed and slammed the door behind her, tinkling the announcing bells loudly.

Daniel jumped out of the truck and hurried over to help her.

"Lucy! Are you okay?" Daniel asked, surprised to see that it was Jed's sister.

"Yes," she said, straightening her long braid and grabbing another bag of chips. "Those Nelwins are such dweebs!"

"You can say that again!" Daniel responded, handing her the last drink container.

"They'll pay!" Her flushed face showed determination.

"Somehow," Daniel sighed. "I just haven't figured out how."

Then Lucy noticed his bandaged head. "How...?"

Daniel motioned his head towards the Nelwins sauntering around inside the café.

"You too?" Lucy glared at them through the window.

Just then Pederson brushed past them and headed into the café. Daniel and Lucy watched him walk over to the counter where the Nelwins sat spinning on stools, sipping on bottles of pop. He spoke to them quietly.

At first the two boys laughed and shook their heads, gesturing at him to leave with flicks of their hands. Pederson barked something at them. A moment later, they both stood up and marched outside in front of the old man, to the amazement of the waitress and several other customers sitting at the tables, solemnly watching them go.

"Let's hear it!" Pederson said quietly.

With slightly embarrassed smirks, Craig and Todd looked at the ground, and mumbled, "Sorry."

"We didn't hear you." Pederson stared at them with cold eyes.

"Sorry we bumped into you," Craig said a little louder.

His smirk disappeared and he looked somewhat contrite.

"Yeah, sorry," Todd echoed, not looking up, clenching his hands at his sides as if he'd like to take a swing at Pederson.

Then he turned to Pederson. "Okay?" he demanded arrogantly. Craig touched Todd on the shoulder as if to calm him down or hold him back.

Pederson looked enquiringly at Lucy. She nodded.

"You boys have yourself a fine day." Pederson said, staring at them coldly.

The two boys shuffled back into the café with their hands in their pockets. As they walked back through the customers, Craig's face seemed flushed and slightly embarrassed, but Todd glared back at anyone daring to look his way.

Lucy grinned at Pederson. "Thanks," she said.

"Anything for a lady," Pederson bowed his head towards her. "May we escort you to your destination?" He held out his bent right arm to her, and with the other took her bag.

Lucy hesitated, and then slid her arm through his. Pederson nodded at Daniel. He took her other arm. Lucy raised her head with dignity, like visiting royalty, and they all sauntered across the street towards the swimming pool. Through the surrounding chain-link fence, they could see her two sisters, Leanne and Lindsay, stop their splashing and watch their approach in amazement.

When Daniel and Pederson released her to go inside

the pool grounds, Lucy curtsied to them and retrieved her grocery bag. Her mom rose from her lawn chair and came to speak to them through the fence. She'd brought the girls in for their swimming lesson.

"Thank you," she said, looking up at Pederson gratefully and tousling Daniel's hair. "I saw what you did for Lucy."

Pederson shrugged. "Those boys need to be taken down a notch or two." He nodded. "Have yourselves a nice day, everyone."

Pederson turned and walked towards the post office. The two younger Lindstrom girls crawled out of the pool, waving at them. Then they gathered around Lucy, who dispersed their snacks. Daniel looked around for Jed.

Mrs. Lindstrom noticed and said, "Jed's lesson is this afternoon. He's gone to Shaunavon with his dad this morning to the Co-op."

"Okay," said Daniel. He wasn't fond of water, and the swimming classes through the school year at Shaunavon were enough for him, but Jed loved the water and would take lessons all summer if he could.

Daniel ran to catch up with Pederson, feeling strangely touched by the old man's kindness and his lack of fear.

When they were back in the truck again, Daniel ventured to ask, "How did you convince them to apologize?"

"I didn't give them a choice, " Pederson answered in a tone Daniel knew meant the subject was closed.

Daniel thought about the events of the day so far. It was barely ten o'clock. What else was going to happen?

They headed down the main street to the old rink, which had become the temporary museum. The Quonset-shaped building had a huge banner across it announcing the "Climax Dinosaur & Historical Museum." The original town museum had moved into the new location, along with the new dinosaur material, in the spring. Everything had been reorganized to incorporate the *Edmontosaurus* information Pederson had discovered.

As they entered the museum, Marlene, a cheerful fifty-year-old volunteer, greeted them.

"Well, if it isn't Ole Pederson and his young protegé, Daniel Bringham."

"Everything going okay?" Pederson asked her.

"Just fine, Ole," she said, straightening up some brochures on the information desk. "We had sixty-five visitors to the museum yesterday."

"Great," he said. "Let's hope there are even more today!"

They took a quick walk through the paleontological part of the museum, heading straight to the replicated *Edmontosaurus* nest and eggs, which had been there since the opening. Pederson had made a name for himself with the discovery. It had been the first nearly totally intact *Edmontosaurus* skeleton, and the only nest of their eggs so far. He'd written a paper on it that had been published in one of the more prestigious paleontology magazines.

They stood in front of the display sign that read "Roxanne," with an explanation of where the *Edmontosaurus* had been found. She was nicknamed Roxanne, a favourite name of Ole Pederson. The full skeleton exhibit was a replica on loan from the Tyrell Museum for the next few years until Pederson's discovery could be fully prepared and examined. Daniel knew this was the usual procedure in museums and that real skeletons were rarely on display.

"They sure did a fine reproduction job!" Pederson said, looking proudly at the nest of sand with a variety of partly hatched eggs and one baby dinosaur crawling up the side.

Daniel noticed the glow of satisfaction on the old man's crinkled face and felt cheered and happy that he'd been part of the experience. He was also incredibly pleased to be part of Pederson's latest digs. Who knew what they would find next!

Pederson nodded at Daniel and silently they both turned and headed to the front desk.

"You're sure you have everything you need, then, Marlene?" Pederson asked.

"All under control," she said with respect.

"All right, then, we'll be off."

On their way out of town, they passed by the little house Pederson used in the wintertime. He also had an old shack in the hills, but it wasn't very protective from the often arcticlike winter weather on the prairies. Even though he preferred working there, his arthritis kept him away; but at the first signs of spring he moved himself totally out to the cabin.

After they passed the tiny town of Frontier, Daniel stared out at the large sloughs, mostly dried up now, but with random islands of pink flowers growing abundantly in them. Maybe there was a similarity between these sloughs and the low-lying marshes of the Cretaceous Period? From what he'd seen, it certainly seemed so.

Once they swung north onto the number 614 grid road, they drove for several miles on gravel again. Grasshoppers swirled up from the ditches of long grass, splatting onto the windshield in a steady barrage along with other flying insects, smudging the glass and making it difficult to see. When the truck wheels hit the pavement again, Daniel heaved a sigh. They were almost at Eastend.

He never ceased to marvel at how the landscape changed from a relatively flat plain and then took a major dip into the valley, with Eastend nestled at the bottom in a long coulee. The town sprawled along the winding Frenchman River amongst a long sweep of lush trees. It had begun in about 1887 as the most eastern detachment from Fort Walsh, a North West Mounted Police (NWMP) post, and was at the east end of their patrol. The name Eastend had stuck, from the constant reference to the location of the post.

Daniel examined the town as they drove in past the Co-op Centre, the Super Thrifty Drug Store, and the grocery store. The extra-wide streets left plenty of room for angle parking on both sides, especially on Main Street. At the end of the block, Pederson parked in front of the Red Coat Booksellers store, one of Daniel's favourite haunts.

"I'll go to the credit union first and meet you back here at the bookstore," Pederson said, heading across the street.

Daniel climbed the steps that led to the bookstore and opened the door. He stood in the doorway breathing in the slightly musty smell of old books, mingled with the crispness of ink and new paper, which he loved. The floor-to-ceiling shelves were loaded with used, new, and rare books on every subject Daniel could imagine. His prime target was the shelf in the back of the store that held all the paleontology books. Many were of a technical nature, some a little too technical for him to read, but that didn't stop him from looking at them. He nodded at the young red-haired woman behind the counter as he passed.

He was so immersed in a book on the evolution of birds that Daniel didn't hear Pederson come in until he spoke behind him.

"Something new, lad?"

Daniel jumped. "Yeah. Look at this!"

Daniel showed him the open page of drawings of successive birdlike species from the prehistoric periods to modern day. Pederson studied if for a moment.

"Hmmm! Some new theories at last." Pederson gently took the book from Daniel and looked at the publication page, then the cover. "Bracken's a good scientist," he said. "Maybe we'll just have to have this one for our library."

Pederson handed the book back to Daniel. "What do you say?"

"Don't buy it just on account of me," Daniel answered, feeling a little guilty at prompting Pederson to buy the book.

"It's for both us!" Pederson answered. "Anything else of interest?"

Daniel shook his head, afraid to speak out again.

"All right, then, we're off."

Soon they were heading across the little bridge over the river and up the winding gravel road to the T.rex Discovery Centre halfway up the valley. The centre had been dug into the side of a hill, following the long natural curve. Actually, the top of the hill had been cut away and then replaced with soil and native plants once the building was complete, so that it looked like it had been entirely carved out of the hillside. All that stuck out was the curved front of the building, done in stone and glass, which looked benevolently over the town of Eastend.

Daniel had been there a couple of times with his school classes, and he and Mr. Pederson had gone once in the early stages of setting up the museum in Climax. Something new was always being added to the displays as the paleontology work was completed.

As they walked around the curved sidewalk to the entrance, Pederson said, "Tim Tokaryk has agreed to meet with me. And so has the Executive Director of the Centre and the Eastend Tourism Authority. Would you like to join us?"

Daniel only took a split second to reach a decision.

"Nah, you go ahead. I'll hang out in the museum."

"I thought so." Pederson nodded knowingly and swung open the big double glass doors. They were greeted by the museum staff, who collected their entrance fees and offered to answer any questions. Pederson explained his mission and was ushered into Mr. Caswell's office, tucked away behind the gift shop.

One of the guides said to Daniel, "The documentary on finding Scotty will start in five minutes, if you're interested."

"Cool," he answered. Even though he'd already seen it with his school class, he wanted to see it again. "I'll be right there."

First, he needed to check something out. Without hesitation he walked into the first section of the museum and peered about. Then he saw it. Hurrying over to a huge footprint display, he squatted down to examine it. Yup! This was what he'd seen, all right!

He compared the length of his arm to the toe impressions, then measured the whole thing by stepping along its length with his feet one in front of the other, his heels butted against the toes of his sneakers. At home he'd measure his feet and calculate how long the impressions were in metric measurements.

When Daniel was sure no one was looking his way, he lay down on the floor and matched himself against it. He remembered how he'd awoken in the past with his head crunched into the depression of the main foot.

There was little doubt he'd been lying in a *Tyrannosaurus rex* footprint!

CHAPTER FIVE

"Are you all right?" asked a dark-haired girl bending over Daniel.

He still lay on the floor beside the *T. rex* footprint, deep in thought. He jumped to his feet.

"Yes, sorry, I was just getting an idea of size." He felt his face go hot.

The girl with the red museum staff T-shirt smiled. "The show is about to start."

Twenty minutes later, Daniel emerged from the theatre contemplating what he'd just seen. Somehow his perspective had changed now that he'd experienced the Cretaceous time personally. He was even more curious to know more about paleontology and what life was really like in the past. Maybe he could set a few records straight!

He never tired of seeing and hearing about the *T. rex* discovery and how they managed to excavate and move the large skeleton to the facility in Eastend. Now it took on new meaning. He could envision what the enormous creature looked like in the flesh and compare it to the massive skeleton left behind.

The museum staff had had to extract Scotty in sections, first deciding where to make each of the four divisions. Then they'd wrapped each piece many times in burlap and plaster to keep it intact. This made the blocks even heavier and more difficult to manipulate. With careful precision, they used a team of Percheron workhorses to turn over the prepared section. Then they wrapped the underside for total preservation. The huge chunks, weighing up to four tonnes, were then loaded onto a flatbed truck, using a large front-end loader. Roxanne had been excavated in much the same way as Scotty, except they hadn't needed to use the horses.

Daniel strolled past the display of a menacing, three-toed *T. rex* foot. He could almost crawl between the toes! No wonder the earth ripped open when one of those creatures walked about.

He headed over to the glass partition that separated the museum from the research station lab. He stared at the huge white blocks of plastered fossils lying on the floor and on shelves that reached the ceiling on one side of the room. He was reading the display cards on the exposed fossils just inside the window, when Pederson and two other men joined him.

"Daniel, you already know Tim Tokaryk. And this is Mark Caswell."

"Nice to see you again, Mr. Tokaryk," said Daniel.

He'd just seen him in the documentary and felt awed to be in his presence again. He'd also seen him a few times at the *Edmontosaurus* dig when he'd come out to help retrieve it, but Daniel hadn't had an opportunity to spend much time with him there.

"Please call me Tim. I'm no different than I was last summer," the well-known paleontologist offered, smiling. He seemed to have noticed Daniel's reverence.

"And pleased to meet you, sir," Daniel said to Mr. Caswell, shaking both men's hands in turn.

"And I'm Mark," Mr. Caswell said in an equally friendly manner.

"Thanks," said Daniel.

They both looked curiously at the bandages on Daniel's head.

"I fell against some rocks," he said, feeling compelled to explain.

"During research?" Mark asked.

"Something like that," Daniel answered, unwilling to describe the real reason.

"Paleontology does have its dangers," Tim said.

Daniel pointed to the lab. "This is awesome!"

"Would you like to have a closer look?" asked Tim.

"As sure as *T. rex*es are carnivores!" Daniel replied, excited at the prospect of seeing the activities up close. Mr. Caswell excused himself, saying he had work to do back in his office. He shook their hands again.

"Please come any time, and if there's anything we can

do for you, we'd be happy to accommodate you. It's always an honour to work with respected paleontologists," said Mark, seeming to include Daniel in his compliment. Then he turned to answer a summons from one of the staff.

Daniel and Mr. Pederson followed Mr. Tokaryk back through the foyer, into an education room and through some doors that said "Staff Only." Daniel wasn't sure what he'd expected, but the paleontologist was no less friendly than he'd been out at their dig. Even in his formal setting, he was just a regular nice guy. Dark, compassionate eyes, glasses, a regular T-shirt and jeans; someone who took the time to talk to a kid! His face, framed by a receding hairline, Fu Manchu moustache, and a light beard, gave a welcoming, knowledgeable, and approachable presence. What a thrill to be in the working lab of the man who had spearheaded the *T. rex* dig!

As they entered the lab, Daniel noticed three work tables, each equipped with large, movable, lighted magnifiers, electrical drills, and a myriad of picks, tools, and brushes. They also were covered with fossils being worked on, and drawings and research information easily accessible at the fingertips of the scientists. A huge exhaust system wound through the room and out of the building.

Fossils, some exposed, and others wrapped in the typical burlap and coated with plaster like huge white rocks, were placed methodically on every conceivable shelf and counter of the spacious room. What was really neat was that visitors to the centre could watch the scientists at work through the glass partition.

Daniel felt privileged to be inside the lab and stood taking all the information in. Much of the equipment was similar to what Pederson had at his home and digs, but this was far more sophisticated and fancy. Pederson seemed impressed too. He looked carefully at the tools, then headed towards the shelves with all the stored fossils.

"The only part of the *T. rex* we've prepared so far is the skull." Tim Tokaryk pointed to the display at the front of the room. "It will take us years to do the whole thing. The skeleton is about sixty-five percent present, and is considered one of the most complete in the world to date. We'll be preparing the limbs next."

"How do you figure Scotty died, Tim?" Daniel asked. *T. rex*es seemed so ferocious and dangerous to all the other creatures of the time that he couldn't imagine something overpowering this top predator. Especially after what he'd seen when he'd somehow gone back into the prehistoric time. What would dare attack a *Tyrannosaurus rex*?

Tim turned to answer Daniel with a thoughtful look. "Hard to say, really. Even if we had completed the investigation, I don't know if we'd know for sure. On first examination, there doesn't appear to be any indication of excessive scarring on the skeleton. No physical reasons. There are no bone injuries, no damage to the skull, or anything of that sort in what's been studied so far."

"What about disease?" Daniel thought to ask.

"Nothing that we're familiar with at this stage," Tim answered. "But anything's plausible – disease, starvation. There would be similar factors to those that face animals today."

Daniel indicated the skull. "Maybe he just died of old age. How old was Scotty?"

Tim laughed. "That's tough too. We think he was probably a young one, maybe like a teenager! He definitely wasn't a full-grown adult, because the skull bones are disassociated, but the skeleton is too large to be a toddler either."

"What does disassociated mean?" Daniel asked.

"Even in humans, when babies are born, there are parts of the skull bones that are not fully attached, which makes the birthing process easier, but as we become older they gradually fill in and develop, along with the growth of the brain, permanent teeth, and changes in facial structure that occur naturally," Tim explained patiently.

"Something similar happens with dinosaurs. By the time they reach early adulthood, all the bones are fused together, and in Scotty's case they are not, so we've deduced he's probably still a young *T. rex.*"

"Cool," Daniel said. "So then it's hard to tell what his death was like?"

"We can tell from where the skeleton was deposited that he died near or in a river system," Tim explained.

"The carcass was trapped in an oxbow type of bend. An overbank may have dropped on top of it, and then the dirt and trees acted like a sieve to help preserve it."

He moved over to the skull on display. "See those?"

"Yeah! Those teeth are deadly!" Daniel said, remembering his private experience when he travelled into the past.

"Kind of like giant bananas," Tim smiled. "Only with edges like steak knives. The tooth is half root and half chomper!"

Daniel laughed. Then he instantly sobered. He'd seen them in action.

Tim continued his explanation, pointing to the jaw. "The gum line keeps the tooth in place. Usually the teeth are shed when we find the skulls. The teeth shoot out with the pressure of the water, but these stayed with the skull, probably because they were trapped by the debris from overhead."

Another man entered, acknowledged the visitors, and began working at one of the tables. Tim introduced him as Wes Long, an RSM technician. Pederson wandered over to examine what he was working and to chat with him.

"We also have several volunteers and other staff members that work here from time to time," Tim explained to Daniel. "We work on other fossils besides Scotty – the crocodile from the Carrot River area, the birdlike creatures, and a new *Mosasaur* find at Diefenbaker Lake."

"Wow!" Daniel's mind whirled; so much going on here that he hadn't realized. Somehow he'd figured they were just concentrating on Scotty's remains. They walked over and looked at the crocodile fossil.

"This crocodile is a much more rare find than Scotty," he noted. "We call him 'Big Bert' and he dates from ninety-two million years ago. By the way, a later relative of this fellow, like the thirty-five to fifty foot, or ten to fifteen metre, *Deinosuchus,* could bring an unsuspecting *T. rex* to its knees. Their behaviour hasn't changed much over the ages. They still lie in wait like logs in the water, although these days the biggest ones are only about twenty feet or six metres long."

As Daniel studied the skeleton, Wes called Tim over to his table to show him something unusual in the plant fossils he worked on. Daniel stood mesmerized in the middle of the lab, thinking again about his wild adventure back in time. He could place all of these creatures in their natural habitat and he felt an awkward moment of terror, as if he was trapped in both times at once. He shook himself as Pederson moved over to join him.

"Well, Daniel, my boy. Seen enough for today?"

"Yes, this is awesome." He studied the drawing of the *T. rex*. "You know they've got this a little wrong, though. The *Tyrannosaurus rex*es have a slightly thinner body right here than that," he commented without thinking. "And their colour is different too."

Daniel stopped when he realized Pederson was giving him a peculiar look. He gulped inwardly and clammed up.

"Why would you say that?" the old man asked curiously.

"Uh..." Daniel's thoughts crashed together. Should he tell Pederson about his adventure? No, that would be introducing too much skepticism about his reliability as an impartial scientist. He wanted people to treat him seriously, not think he was a kid making up stories.

Just then Tim returned and Daniel blurted out, "Do you think it would ever be possible to go back in time to see what the Cretaceous world was all about?"

"I suppose anything's possible, Daniel, but figuring out how to do it and then proving it would be the challenge," he answered seriously. "Although you might find it a little outdated, you might want to read a book by George Gaylord Simpson, called the *Dechronization of Sam Magruder*. It's a story written by an eminent scientist before his death in 1984. He exerted a major influence on bringing paleontology into the modern theory of evolution. In the story, he goes back into prehistoric time."

Pederson nodded his head. "I've read it. I have a copy of it that you can borrow, Daniel."

"Thanks," Daniel said, avoiding Pederson's inquiring gaze. Then he abruptly changed the subject again and addressed Tim. "How well do you think *T. rex*es could see?"

"The latest theory is that they had stereoscopic vision. This means they could see things in full 3D."

Daniel gulped and stared, deep in thought.

Tim took his reaction to be one of misunderstanding, and explained, "That means they could see three dimensionally, and quite well."

"Interesting," Pederson said. "Quite the opposite of what Magruder thought in the book you mentioned. That fellow thought," he explained to Daniel, "that their eyesight was poor and that all you had to do was jump off to the side of their field of vision. Sort of like you blended into the background or you could be almost underfoot, but they couldn't spot you."

Sure wish that was so, Daniel said to himself. He was sure it was pure luck that kept the *T. rex* he'd encountered from seeing him.

"What about their sense of smell?" he asked, curious now.

"Hard to say," said Tim, "but I suspect they had a heightened awareness. Some scientists liked to think they ate strictly carrion – already dead animals. That's because of their top-heavy weight and tiny forearms, which some think made it impossible for them to pursue or capture live prey," Tim explained. "Others argue that they used their massive tails for balance during the chase, and their awesome jaws to subdue supper."

After seeing the *T. rex* hunting the *Edmontosaurus*, Daniel knew the one set of scientists were dead wrong. He'd seen it move at tremendous speed for its weight, destroying everything in its path. Daniel brought his attention back to Tim's account.

"I'm sure they wouldn't walk away from a free meal, but I'm sure they also hunted for their own feasts and weren't just scavengers. I suspect that they could detect all sorts of animals – reptiles, mammals, rodents, etc. – with their good sense of smell.

"You mean, maybe they could even smell humans?" Daniel asked apprehensively.

"You bet!" Pederson said with another quizzical look at Daniel.

"Humans are mammals, right? So indeed they could. You'd make a nice mouthful," Tim joked. "One snap and you'd be gone! They had very strong jaws."

Daniel felt himself go rigid with remembered fear.

Tim seemed to notice, because he added, "I'm sure they were more interested in the larger herbivores, though."

"Like an *Edmontosaurus!*" Daniel thought again of the *T. rex*'s terrorizing kill. How fortunate he was to be alive!

"Exactly," Pederson and Tim said simultaneously.

"They were complete bullies. They picked on everything and they had the size and meanness to do it!" Pederson said, lifting his eyebrows. "Sounds like some people we know!"

Daniel gave Pederson a tight smile, remembering the Nelwins' behaviour.

"It's amazing how humans can reflect animal behaviour," Tim said, raising his eyebrows in an understanding way.

"Well, Daniel, my boy, time we were off," suggested

Pederson. "I'm sure Mr. Tokaryk has more important things to do than chat with us all day."

"No problem," Tim said sincerely, "I always enjoy an enquiring young mind."

Just then Daniel's stomach rumbled. "Guess I am hungry," he admitted with a grin.

"We'll head to town then." Pederson turned to Tim. "Thanks so much for your assistance." He shook his hand. "Seems like museums are a little more approachable than in my early days."

"I'd like to think they're a little more open-minded," replied Tim. "Give me a call any time."

With a quick nod, Tim returned to his work table covered with bird fossils and a stack of phone messages. Daniel and Pederson made their way out through the labyrinth of fossils and counters.

"Wow, that was awesome," he repeated again as soon as they were out of the building.

"Sure was!" Pederson agreed as they walked to the parking lot under the beating rays of the hot sun.

"So what did they say about the business idea?" Daniel asked, striding to keep up to Pederson and scanning the scrubby hillsides. He was always on the lookout for interesting markings or protrusions.

Pederson said, "They gave me some great information and they're willing to link us to their operation and on their Web site."

"Great!"

"We still have a pile of work to do and quite a few hurdles to go through before we're ready for that stage," Pederson said, climbing into the truck and turning the ignition.

Daniel jumped into the truck and slammed the door. "I'm sure we can do it!" he said, waiting for Pederson to explain the steps.

"How about if I go over it all with you and your parents when we get back? Right now, I'm parched and a might peckish too." Pederson reversed out of the parking lot.

Daniel hid his disappointment. Instead, he focused on all he'd seen and heard that day. The more information he took in, the more questions seemed to pop up.

At least now he knew for sure the *T. rex* could have sussed him out through sight and smell and made dinner out of him in one snap of his immense mouth. If it hadn't already been preoccupied with preying on the *Edmontosaurus*, there was no telling what might have happened. But from what Daniel had learned, there wasn't any way to tell if that *T. rex* was actually Scotty.

As they drove along, he had a feeling that Pederson was suspicious about his holding back something. Should he tell him? He sure wanted to talk it over with someone. But what if Pederson laughed? Or worse, what if he thought Daniel was just a dumb kid and decided that he didn't want to have him around anymore?

"All right, young man, what's up?" asked Pederson in his gruff, no-nonsense way.

Instantly, Daniel felt his whole body tense with dread.

"What do you mean?" he asked as innocently as he could. His voice came out barely above a whisper.

"There's something you know that you're not telling." Pederson pulled into a parking spot on the main street, down a few yards from Jack's Café. Pederson turned to him. "What was that all about when you mentioned the shape of the body and the colour of the *T. rex*?"

"I'm not sure I know what you mean." Daniel stalled for time. His palms were sweaty and he quickly wiped them on the legs of his jeans.

Pederson turned and glared at him.

"Out with it, lad!"

CHAPTER SIX

Daniel stammered, "I-I-I'm not sure if I should say anything."

"Why ever not?" Pederson asked, turning off the engine.

"Well, it's a little unbelievable, even to me!" Daniel tapped his feet nervously, and stared straight ahead.

"Daniel!" Pederson was obviously exasperated.

"Fine!" He plunged into his story, staring out the windshield. "What if I told you I actually went back into prehistoric time?"

Silence.

"That I actually experienced what it was like?"

More silence. Daniel peeked at Pederson out of the corner of his eyes. Pederson stroked his beard, and seemed lost in thought.

"It happened when the Nelwins knocked me to the ground and I hit my head."

Pederson grunted. His fingers stopped moving.

Daniel faced him. "Well, say something," he said.

RAP! RAP! An elderly woman with a wizened face stepped up to Pederson's side of the truck and rapped again on his door with her metal cane.

"Ole Pederson! I don't believe it's you, in the flesh!"

"Why, Mildred Roost!" Pederson stared at the tall woman in surprise.

She had an Australian outback hat squashed onto her long, grey, braided hair. A faded plaid cotton shirt topped a pair of baggy sweatpants, both of which hung loosely over her rather plump body. She grinned at him, asking, "What brings you to these parts?"

"I could ask you the same."

"I'm here with the University of Alberta Paleontology Department. We hope to work on a joint project with the Royal Saskatchewan Museum," she divulged.

"I am in a way too," Pederson answered. The RSM had assisted with the retrieval and now the preparation of the *Edmontosaurus*.

"Geez, that's right, Ole. How could I forget? You found that hadrosaur with the nest and eggs. It was around here somewhere, wasn't it!" She peered at Daniel. "Who's that, a grandson?" she asked. "No, sorry, I remember now. You and your wife never had children. Who is he, then?" she demanded, not stopping to let either of them answer the questions.

Pederson raised his eyebrows in slight annoyance and then he introduced Daniel. "He's my young protegé and esteemed colleague. Daniel Bringham, meet Dr. Mildred Roost."

Daniel nodded in acknowledgement, and puffed his chest up with pride. Pederson considered him a colleague!

"How do you do, ma'am," Daniel said sincerely.

"A boy with manners! I like you already, young man!" She tapped her cane on the door again. "Well, get on out of there, you two. Let's go have some lunch. It's on me."

She stomped over to the sidewalk, using her cane to propel herself along. Daniel and Pederson looked at each other and got out of the truck.

"We'll eat there," she said, pointing to Jack's Café. "Best food in town. Their garlic toast is a secret recipe. So is their house salad dressing. Talk about 'valley of hidden secrets.' Everything about this community is one of the best-kept secrets from the rest of the world. But the locals are great about sharing!"

She pointed to the dinosaur footprints painted on the sidewalk. "They lead you right where you want to go!"

Seemed there was no getting away from this woman. Daniel smiled as he watched Pederson meekly follow her instructions. The woman was a bit of a bully, but the old man didn't seem to take offence. They headed into Jack's Café.

"Some things are just better to go along with than cause trouble," he said later when they were back on the road.

The woman had talked non-stop, filling Pederson in on all the latest developments in the Alberta paleontology world, including news about the various people they both knew. Daniel sighed in relief as he listened to the barrage. Mildred Roost had given him a reprieve from telling Pederson his weird story, but the tide turned again when they were back on the highway.

"Okay, young man, let's hear the rest of your story!" Pederson said, concentrating on his driving,

"First, tell me what you think so far," Daniel said, fidgeting in his seat. He ran his right hand up and down the seat belt that ran across his shoulder. "Sounds like you think it's just some *story* I'm making up."

"I know you better than that, lad," said Pederson. "I'm not sure what to make of it just yet. Anything is possible – something could have altered your state of mind when you hit your head..."

"See, I knew it," Daniel interrupted. "You think it's all because I hit my head."

"Or it could have been a dream state, some sort of delusion from the bump on the head..." Pederson continued patiently as if Daniel hadn't interrupted.

"But, but..." Daniel protested, straining the seat belt as he turned to Pederson.

"No, let me finish, " Pederson continued kindly. "Or there is a possibility you really did go back in time through some sort of shift in reality. Now, if that's the case, we need to have proof. Remember, we are scientists."

Daniel settled back, somewhat deflated, yet not altogether discouraged.

"First, we need to examine each of the possibilities from various perspectives to eliminate those that didn't happen," Pederson explained. "Then we need to test the one we think is the right answer. Fair enough?" He turned to look at Daniel.

Daniel nodded and thought about the possibilities. "So you might just believe me?"

"Let's do our research and then I'll give you my opinion," Pederson suggested.

"Okay," Daniel said reluctantly. Man, this could take a long time. How was he ever going to prove it to Pederson? At least the old man hadn't laughed him out of the truck, or told him he was a flake and that he never wanted to work with him again.

Daniel took a deep breath and told Pederson the rest of the story. When he finished, Pederson nodded. "Thank you, Daniel. I can see we've got a lot to think about." Daniel relaxed, glad he'd told someone.

"Look!" Pederson pointed to the valley on their right.

Several antelope were crossing a ravine down below them, headed towards a small stream. Pederson slowed and they watched them for several minutes until they drank and disappeared into a bluff of trees. For the next few miles Daniel and Pederson were silent, each caught up in their own thoughts as they watched the passing landscape.

As they neared Shaunavon, pumpjacks over oil wells began popping up everywhere across the countryside, even several close together on some people's land. Daniel considered again how lucky he had been that his family hadn't been forced to go that route. Although the fields looked fine now, with crops surrounding the pumpjacks, he knew there had been seismic testing, and roads cut through the land, while the drilling crews brought in the necessary equipment.

At the time he hadn't understood all the rigmarole, but he knew there had been a bit of a tussle with the Crown for some people in the area, as they didn't hold all the mineral rights on their land. Only some of those who had original homesteaded land managed to own the mineral rights, which included oil and gas. Everyone else had only what was called "surface rights." Even though they'd bought and paid for their land, they only owned the surface, not the mines and minerals below! Daniel still couldn't believe it.

"Tell me again how that could have worked about us being forced to give our land over for mineral rights," he said.

"Your family didn't have to, Daniel, because your great-grandfather homesteaded it and owned those rights. They were printed right on his land title papers. Even so, your parents could have signed them over if they'd wanted to, but because we'd proved there were heritage prospects in the form of fossils on the land, they chose not to."

"Okay, but what happened to Jed's family? How come they had to fight against the testing?"

Patiently, Pederson explained. "They didn't own the rights in the first place, but they can refuse to allow the oil companies on their property, which they did, because they wanted to preserve the land, as you know." Pederson looked over at him and smiled in a conspiratorial way. "They have some crazy idea that they might have dinosaur fossils on their property too."

Daniel grinned.

Pederson looked back at the road and continued his main explanation. "Then the decision goes to arbitration, which means a group of people act like a jury and discuss the situation. They make the decision as to whether or not the companies get to drill."

"It seemed to me they had to talk to a lot of important people." Daniel noted.

"Yes, the Conservation Data Centre, the Heritage Resource Impact people, and the Saskatchewan Environment and Resource Management team is contacted and are all brought into the discussion."

Daniel said, "Okay, I think I understand now. Basically, the area is scanned for endangered plants and animals, and for archaeological and environmental aspects, before anything can happen?"

"You've got it! If any of those areas are at risk because of the seismic testing and future drilling, then it's not likely going to happen," Pederson explained. "If there's a good reason, such as some sort of heritage element – an important burial ground or foundations of special old buildings, paleontology possibilities, or something along that line, then they can be excused."

"So, because Jed's family didn't have anything like that, they had to let the testing be done?" Daniel asked.

"Exactly. The pumpjacks will go in later this month. They'll be paid for the use of the land as well as an annual rental for the right to drill and produce wells on their land. It won't make them rich, but it will help out."

"So maybe Jed's dad won't have to go to the city to work this winter?"

"Maybe not," Pederson acknowledged, keeping his eyes on the road.

"Cool. Jed hates it when his father's gone. He's in a houseful of bossy girls!"

Daniel and Pederson laughed.

"I don't think it's necessarily because they're girls!" Pederson said. "I know a few bossy boys too!" Pederson gave him a significant look, remembering how Daniel had saved him in the snowstorm two winters before.

A few minutes later, Daniel asked, "What would have happened, say, if my parents had said yes?"

"If oil had been found, they would have received a royalty payment based on the production of the well or wells. Maybe something like $2,000 each a year for the rental on the surface leases. They'd get an additional amount, which would fluctuate according to oil prices. So depending on how many wells they had and how long they ran for, they could have made a tidy sum over the years."

Yikes, Daniel hadn't realized that! They might have been almost rich! He wondered how his parents felt about that. A sudden sinking feeling hit the pit of his stomach like a chunk of apple he hadn't chewed properly. Maybe he shouldn't have been so insistent about them not signing the papers. But what good would the money have done, if the fossil history had been destroyed? He twisted and turned these new thoughts over in his mind. No wonder his parents had been so reluctant to consider his suggestions. They'd made a real sacrifice to go along with his plans!

When Pederson turned left into Shaunavon and pulled up to the grocery store, Daniel barely noticed they'd stopped. He wondered if what he'd convinced his parents to do had been the right thing. Surely they wouldn't have gone along with it, if they hadn't agreed?

"I just need a few items. Anything you'd like, Daniel?" Pederson asked stepping down from the truck.

"Uh, yeah, let me think. There was something Mom wanted." Daniel couldn't remember.

"Well maybe if you come in and look around you'll think of it," Pederson offered.

Daniel followed him inside. His family grew most of their own vegetables and raised their own meat, so he avoided those aisles, and the junk food. He knew she shouldn't want any of that! Then he saw it. Twelve loaves of bread on sale! His mom rarely baked bread in the summertime for the family, as the weather was just too hot, and she especially preferred to buy bread for all the sandwiches she would make for the tourists' day trip lunches and the toast for their breakfasts. They had a huge freezer at home, so Daniel gathered up six loaves of bread in each hand, half white and half whole wheat, and headed for the checkout counter.

Forty-five minutes later, they were back home.

"Tell your folks I'll come over after dinner and we'll discuss what I found out today," Pederson said as Daniel jumped down from the truck and gathered the bread. "You might ask them to give the Lindstroms a call, and invite them over too."

"Will do," said Daniel, nodding his head as he clutched the bread in his hands and tried not to squish it.

Pederson still didn't have a phone and had no intention of getting one. He preferred to walk most places too, except when he had to make a trip into town for supplies, or when he was hauling something too heavy to carry on his back.

As Daniel rounded the shady side of the house, Dactyl arose, stretching and yawning, then padded over to Daniel and followed him to the back porch. Mom met him at the door and grabbed some of the bread as it slid from his sweaty hands.

"Thanks, Daniel," she said, holding the screen door open for him.

He gave Dactyl a quick pet and went inside. Cheryl stood in the kitchen doorway, gurgling at the sight of him. She walked over to him on chubby legs; her blonde curls bouncing around her smiling face. Daniel scooped her in his arms and gave her a big hug.

"Mr. Pederson's coming over after dinner to tell you about his meeting. He wants us to call the Lindstroms too. I can call, if you like," he offered, wanting to speak to Jed anyway.

"Sure, go ahead, Daniel," she said. "Tell them to come about seven o'clock."

Daniel carried Cheryl over to the phone on the wall in the kitchen.

"Jedlock!" he said when his friend answered. He explained his reason for calling.

While Jed set down the phone to talk to his parents, Daniel tickled Cheryl until she squirmed and almost slid out of his arms. She was getting heavier all the time, so he stopped and set her onto the floor. She padded away to get the carrot stick Mom held out to her.

"Mom, can Jed come for supper?" Daniel asked on the spur of the moment.

"Sure," she answered, turning back to the kitchen sink to peel more carrots.

Jed returned to the other end of the phone.

"No problemo," he said. "My folks will be there."

"Good, how about you coming now and you can stay for supper?"

"Hang on!"

He could hear Jed calling to his mom in another room of their house.

When he came back, he said, "Sure, I have to do a few chores first, though, then I'll bike over. Say in about an hour and a half?"

"Sure. See ya soon!

"Okay!" Jed slammed down the receiver in Daniel's ear like he always did.

Daniel headed to the fridge for some cool water, drank two glasses full, and then headed outside. It was too early to start chores. And he sure didn't want to be roped into doing any more than he had to. He plodded over to the garden and into the raspberry patch. His mom couldn't see him from the window.

He'd eaten a couple of handfuls, when he suddenly remembered he needed to go back to his hideout. He'd seen a display of plant fossil impressions at the museum, and it reminded him of something peculiar on the piece of bark that lay on his hideout floor. Quickly, Daniel headed to the house and called to his mother through the screen in the kitchen window.

"Mom, I'm going to my hideout for a really short while. I just need to put a couple of things away," he said.

"Come and get your hat and some water," Mom insisted.

Daniel screwed up his face, "Aw, Mom, I won't be gone long!"

"You won't be going at all unless you get your hat and some water!" she retorted.

Daniel mumbled to himself as he gathered the items, along with his backpack and research book. He already had his rock hammer sticking out of his back pocket. Jamming his baseball cap on his head, he whistled for Dactyl and they headed off at a fairly quick pace. He wanted to make sure he was back in time to meet Jed. This time there were no games with his dog. Dactyl seemed to sense the urgency and stayed close to his heels. Besides, it was too hot to do chasing of any kind.

The sun was still high in the sky and hot as ever. Daniel was secretly glad his Mom had made him bring the water. As he walked he took an irregular path, keeping his eyes out for the Nelwins, but they didn't seem to be around.

Daniel reached his hideout without incident and crawled into the somewhat cooler interior. He removed his backpack and dug out a bottle of water, and took a couple of swigs while Dactyl did his usual examination of the entire cavern. Then he poured some water in the old tin pot for his pet. Right after that, Daniel put the water bottle into his backpack and at the same time picked up the piece of bark off the floor.

Instantly, there was a crackling noise, and then Dactyl and the cave disappeared!

CHAPTER SEVEN

Daniel froze. "Oh, no! Not again!!!"

He stood in shallow, reedy water, staring at a prehistoric forest. Eerily, a low mist shrouded the tops of the trees. He looked desperately around for any signs of immediate danger. Seeing nothing he recognized, he examined his situation.

In one hand he held his backpack and in the other the chunk of bark from his hideout floor. He looked down at his feet. Luckily he had his runners on, as there were all kinds of bugs and strange things floating on the water. Who knew what they were or if they'd bite or sting? Or what else might be lurking in the depths? He looked about quickly and stepped as fast as he dared onto the marshy shore. Every nerve in his body tingled and his chest tightened with each step he took.

Weird, piercing calls sounded from deep within the trees. Behind him the landscape was desolate and swampy with little fingers of land along the edges.

Numerous small islands with a few trees and plants on them spotted the shallow sea. Small groupings of water lilies floated a few yards from the shore. The air smelled just like it did back home after a rain.

As he walked over the muddy ground, his sneakers made sucking noises every time he lifted a foot. Little sand creatures scurried out of his way and hundreds of minnows swam in shallow puddles. Giant dragonflies fluttered by on translucent yellow wings, and distorted-looking bees droned about the low flowering magnolias. The white blossoms gave off a strong perfumed scent that made him sneeze as he headed towards the denser trees and more solid ground. And, he hoped, to some kind of safety!

As he rounded a bluff of trees, he stopped short. A huge carcass lay in torn shreds and rotting hunks over the ground in front of him. Small animals and birdlike creatures swooped in, ripped off portions, and scurried away with them, oblivious to Daniel. He looked more closely at the frame of the dead dinosaur. It was a *Stegosaurus.* He could tell by what was left of the dome-shaped head. The *Edmontosaurus* must have escaped! He felt only slightly cheered by the thought.

Holding his nose to keep out the smell of rotting flesh, he picked his way through the leftover debris. He noted the huge tooth marks made by the *T. rex* when it attacked, killed, and ripped apart its prey. His thoughts turned to Roxanne and he wondered if there had been any progress on the cleaning and preparation of their special find. How had Roxanne died?

A rustling sound from the other side of the trees brought Daniel back to instant alertness. With extreme care, he skirted the debris in a wide arc, hiding behind various clumps of low bushes. He headed towards a small stand of shorter trees, where he examined the cycad ferns beneath them. When he was sure there were no nests or other creatures inhabiting the foliage, he crawled under the fronds and sat against their base. Whew! He'd made it!

Good thing there were ferns. He sure didn't relish climbing one of the giant redwoods at the moment. If anything, the air seemed even hotter and moister than in the previous visit, Daniel thought, wiping the sweat from his face.

As he reached for his backpack for some water, he realized he still held the piece of bark. He examined the thick, reddish-brown, rough texture. How had he ended up with it at his hideout? Where had it come from? He was sure he'd never seen it before he'd been in dinosaur time. And for sure, it wasn't from a local tree around his farm. They were all poplars, willows, and elms, not forest conifers.

He peered about and held the bark between his fingers in the air, comparing it to a nearby redwood tree. From this distance, it appeared to be similar. Slowly he stuck his head out of the ferns and checked for danger, and then he crawled from his hiding place. Upright again, he headed for the tree. No doubt about it. The bark belonged to a redwood.

Just then the ground started to tremble beneath his feet. Something huge was approaching. At first he couldn't tell from which direction, but as the vibrations increased, they seemed to be coming from the forest in front of him and to his left. What to do? Dive back under the fern or climb the tree? He chose the fern. There wasn't time to scale up any trunks.

The ground shook beneath him as he ran back to the fern. He startled a small dog-sized lizard and nearly tripped. But he managed to get under the fern and tight against the base before whatever creature it was appeared. Moments later he saw a *Tyrannosaurus!* Its huge yellow eyes glared out of its ferocious head that swung twenty feet above Daniel. Somehow it seemed even more terrifying now that he'd examined the skeleton closely at the Discovery Centre. Daniel was probably nothing more to the *T. rex* than a barn cat would be to him!

Even though it was still several yards away from him, the ground vibrated in waves with each step it took. Daniel tightened his mouth to keep his teeth from chattering. He trembled all over! The *T. rex*'s huge feet left deep indentations in the mud as it headed towards the sea. As it passed, Daniel saw the scar on its back. It was the same *T. rex* from before! He'd definitely come back to the same time and almost the same place! How could this have happened?

Thinking back to the first time he'd travelled back to the Cretaceous Period, Daniel recalled how he'd climbed the redwood and then been attacked by the *Pteranodon*. When he'd returned home and emptied his backpack, the bark had fallen out. A piece must have broken off and fallen into his pack when he fell from the tree!

He stared at the piece still clutched in his hand. Had he gone back in time again when he'd picked it up? That must be it! It was the last thing he'd touched before he'd been transferred into the prehistoric world. Obviously he'd carried it around in his backpack and nothing had happened, but as soon as he came into physical contact with it, the shift had occurred! Did that mean the opposite would happen? If he let go of the bark, would he return to his own time?

Before he could decide, the *T. rex* swung about and headed in his direction. It snorted and swung its head about as if it were sniffing a scent in the air. Daniel felt his mouth drop open. Had it detected him? Was he going to be lunch? This time there were no distractions for the creature as it plodded his way. Daniel gasped and shrunk into the shrubbery, but there was nowhere to hide from a vicious dinosaur. Its huge feet covered a large area of ground in a short time and the ground quaked.

So did Daniel! In a total panic of clashing nerves and rolling stomach, Daniel couldn't think straight. He clutched his backpack and moved backwards just as the *T. rex*'s head dropped to inspect the fern he hid under.

Without even realizing it, Daniel dropped the chunk of bark inside his backpack. A loud snapping noise cracked in his ear.

Instantly, he was back in the present – a few yards from his hideout. Inside, he heard Dactyl let out a howl. Daniel ducked inside. His eyes had gone blurry, but he could just make out the shape of Dactyl, cowering in the back of the cave.

"It's okay, boy," he said, trembling uncontrollably from the narrow escape. Gradually his eyes cleared.

His teeth chattered and every nerve in his body seemed to tingle at once. Daniel flung the backpack off. It landed a couple of feet away. Then he thumped onto the ground and sat there. Dactyl whined and slowly came forward to examine him, licking his face and wagging his tail. Daniel raised his arm and hugged his dog to him tightly. He'd thought he might never see him again.

Even though the hideout was warm and cozy, Daniel couldn't stop shivering. He knew it was from shock, but he wasn't sure what to do about it. He wasn't even sure if he could walk home again. He needed a drink of water, but he was afraid to touch the backpack. Something told him to stay clear of the piece of bark, which he vaguely recalled he'd dropped back inside at the last possible second. He could still feel and smell the horrible breath of the *T. rex*!

Then he thought about the surprise the *T. rex* must have had when he'd disappeared before its startled "3D" eyes. As he tried to imagine the astonished look on its fiercely grotesque face, he began laughing hysterically. Dactyl began barking in excitement. When he gained control again, Daniel sat up and wiped the tears from his eyes. He was parched.

Slowly, he crawled over to his backpack and touched it. Nothing happened, so he carefully opened a flap. He saw the chunk of bark, and licking his lips in deep concentration, he avoided it while he drew a bottle of water from the pack. Relaxing when he had the bottle safely in his hands, he took a long drink, letting the refreshing moisture soothe his dry throat. He swirled it around his mouth and closed his eyes, savouring it. He was grateful for being alive and being able to taste and swallow. If things had gone differently, the *T. rex* would be swallowing *him* right now! Scotty or not, that beast was not a friendly one!

When he finished, he set the bottle on the cave floor and with great delicacy tipped the rest of the contents out of the backpack. Using the handle of his rock hammer, he separated everything away from the piece of bark, being careful not to touch it. Dactyl went over to sniff at it.

Daniel hollered at him. "No, boy! Don't touch!" He brushed Dactyl away roughly.

Dactyl whined and looked eagerly at Daniel, wagging his tail in short bursts of confusion. Daniel poured some water in Dactyl's dish to distract him. Now he had to think of a safe place to keep the bark. He should have left it behind and then there wouldn't have been any more trouble. If only he'd thought of that then!

But he knew, somewhere deep inside him, that he had too much curiosity and that maybe sometime, if he planned properly, he'd go back again to explore. For right now, though, he didn't want the bark to fall into the wrong hands. Nor did he want Dactyl touching it, in case it affected him too.

Then a crazy thought struck him. Pederson wanted proof. Maybe he'd give him the opportunity! He shook his head as if to clear his thoughts. The time shift must have addled his brain. He didn't want to subject the old man to such a horrible encounter. He might have a heart attack or something. There wasn't anyone he could share the adventure with – Jed would be needlessly traumatized too.

Suddenly, Daniel remembered that Jed would be over soon. He had to get back! He collected his belongings into his backpack and stared at the bark. He didn't dare touch it – not even to move it with a stick. Maybe if he just covered it somehow. He looked around the hideout and spotted a pot lid. Perfect for now! He placed it over top, careful not to disturb the chunk in any way.

He breathed a sigh of relief and headed for the doorway. At least he'd quit shaking, although he still felt a little chilled. Dactyl had already bounded out and was heading up the hillside, sniffing at the ground.

As Daniel reached the farmyard, he saw Jed pedalling his bike down the lane beside the house and waved to him.

"Jedlock! Over here!"

Jed waved back. He jumped off his bike and leaned it against a shed. They met in the middle of the yard next to the outdoor kitchen and concession stand that had been remodelled from an old shed to serve tour guests breakfast.

"Geeze, it's hot today!" Jed said, taking off his baseball cap. His fair hair was matted to his head.

"Yeah," Daniel replied, even though he enjoyed the heat of the sun beating down on him. At least he wasn't shivering anymore.

"Come on," he said, "I happen to know my mom was baking cookies for tonight and we have some cold Gatorade too."

Refreshed, Daniel and Jed saddled up Gypsy and Pepper. They needed to be exercised anyway. Besides, Daniel didn't feel like any more vigorous activity and Jed had just pedalled a couple of miles down a gravel road.

"Let's go see the campsite first," Jed suggested.

Their dads were doing the final preparations for the first tourists on the weekend. The boys followed the trail through the yard and across the pasture. Grasshoppers whizzed at them from all sides, so they did little talking at first, by silent consent. They weren't taking any chances on swallowing one of the flying insects. It had happened before.

Daniel grinned at the memory. He'd gagged and spit and torn at his mouth as the grasshopper tried to escape. He'd pulverized it unintentionally, and for weeks afterwards he'd kept swallowing at something imaginary stuck in his throat.

He gestured at Jed, pointing at the grasshoppers and then making a zipping motion over his mouth. Jed grinned back at him, holding his mouth tight. Gypsy and Pepper flicked at the insects with their tails and plodded along the grassy trail.

Then they took a dip down a slight incline and rounded a curve. At the bottom of the hill they could see the tree-filled coulee and hear the pounding of posts. They rousted their horses to a slightly faster pace. When they reached the cool shade of the trees, they dismounted and led their horses to a trickling stream, where they tied them to a couple of low trees so they could reach both the water and the grass.

"Hello, boys," Doug Lindstrom, Jed's dad, greeted them, as he manoeuvred another post into a hole in the ground and Daniel's dad pounded it in solidly with a sledgehammer.

They had created a circle of posts to designate a parking area between the camping and picnicking spots.

They'd built several tables and set them in strategic places under the shade of the trees. Then they'd cleared out a dozen or so camping spots with just enough room in each for a tent or a small trailer.

A water well with a hand pump stood between the two areas at the edge of the parking lot. Two outhouses – outdoor bathrooms – were tucked behind some trees in the camping area. Daniel had torn down an old bin for the lumber for them. When their dads had finished building them, Daniel had painted them. He looked at them now with pride, fresh white with green trim.

"You boys here to give us a hand?" Dad asked. "Nah, I didn't think so," he guessed before they could answer.

"What do you need done?" Jed asked, always ready to help.

"We have a little time before I have get back to do chores," Daniel agreed reluctantly.

"You could gather up those branches and put them on the back of the truck," Dad suggested. He pointed to a huge pile they'd cleared when they carved the beginning of the hiking trail that led into the camping area.

Daniel sighed. Just what he needed! He grimaced at Jed, who looked as crestfallen as he felt.

"You and your big mouth!" Daniel whispered at him jokingly.

"Sorry," Jed answered, as his dad went to back the truck closer for them.

They worked quickly, stacking the branches into the

truck box, and a half-hour later they were finished. Sweat poured down their faces and their T-shirts clung to their backs. Their arms were all scratched, red, and itchy. Mercifully, not too many mosquitoes had bitten them.

"Good job, boys," Dad said, striding over to take a look.

"Yes, you two are good workers!" Jed's dad agreed. "Fast, too. You must have time for something else."

"No way! We're out of here!" Daniel said. "I still have chores to do!" And his head was beginning to throb.

"Yeah, we haven't had any time to ourselves yet!" Jed complained.

Their dads laughed.

"We were only joking," Dad said.

"Good," Daniel said, heading towards the horses. "Come on, Jed. Let's get out of here before they change their minds!"

Astride the saddles again, Daniel and Jed headed across country, around the coulee and up a different side of the hill. That's when they spotted a couple of figures in the distance, peering down at them from the top of the hill.

"Bet it's the Nelwins!" Daniel yelled, urging Gypsy faster. "Come on, let's check it out!"

Jed, on Pepper, followed close behind. Whoever it was ahead was on foot, so they should be able to catch up to them in no time. However, moments later, when they reached the top, they couldn't see anyone. There were so many coulees and dips in the hills in that particular area that the two people could have gone in any direction.

"Darn! It's not worth looking for them," Daniel said, reining Gypsy in and turning to face Jed. "But I'm sure it was the Nelwins spying on us."

Daniel told Jed about his encounter with them the day before. He left out the part about going back into prehistoric time. He still wasn't ready to tell anyone the details of that experience.

"I heard what you and Pederson did for Lucy, too," Jed said. "Sure wish there were something we could do about that pair!"

"I'm sure there is. We just need to come up with a plan."

"Yeah, right!" Jed mumbled. "Got any great ideas?"

"Well, I might," Daniel said, thinking about the piece of redwood bark. No! That would be too mean! And too dangerous! He just wanted them to stop their bullying. He didn't want to injure or kill them.

"I'll think it through before I say anything," he said quietly.

Jed said, "Okay, count me in, whatever it is!"

Daniel just hoped he didn't have to do anything!

CHAPTER EIGHT

Daniel opened the door to Ole Pederson, who arrived before the Lindstroms that night. He held a book in his hand for Daniel.

"The one Tim Tokaryk recommended to you this morning," Pederson said.

Daniel took the book in surprise. "Thanks. That was fast!"

Pederson patted Daniel on the shoulder. "No time like the present, I always say!" He had an excited glint in his eyes that Daniel recognized. It meant Pederson had a viable plan for the paleontology dig. He could hardly wait to hear it!

He led Pederson into the dining room where Mom had set out a tray of chocolate chip cookies and saskatoon muffins, and two jugs of iced tea on the table. Dad sat at the end of the table opposite from the stack of glasses and napkins. He had his usual array of papers spread out, along with a calculator and various coloured pens and pencils.

Pederson sat around the corner from him as Dad passed him a paper with a chart drawn on it with coloured lines. Jed and Daniel slid onto chairs near them to hear the discussion. Cheryl played with a cookie in her high-chair beside Jed, who made funny faces at her.

"Evening, Ole! Good to see you!" Dad said. "Here are my projections for the year. Of course, these aren't set in solid stone. We can still chip away at it."

Jed and Daniel groaned at Dad's attempt to make a paleontology-related pun.

"Well, Ed, we may just have to change these projections a little." Pederson said. "But let's wait for the others so I don't repeat myself!"

"How about some iced tea?" Mom asked, standing behind him with the jug and a glass in her hand. She nodded at Daniel to pass the tray of desserts.

"Don't mind if I do!" he said, accepting a glass from Mom.

Daniel grabbed the tray and offered it to Mr. Pederson and then Dad. Jed stood beside him with the napkins. That's when the Lindstroms arrived. Jed's mom, Greta, sailed into the dining room.

"My, aren't we the helpful host?" she teased Jed, setting down a plate of cherry squares.

Jed blushed and rolled his eyes at his mom. His three sisters entered next and took their places respectfully at the table. Their dad brought up the rear, as usual.

"Evening, everyone," Doug Lindstrom said in a jolly

mood, and scraped a chair across the floor and sat on the other side of Daniel's dad.

All at once the room filled with chattering and laughter as everyone talked at the same time. Once the greetings and small talk were over and everyone had been served, they focused their attention on Ole Pederson.

"Well, everyone, as you know the townspeople and community around Climax have rallied together and we have the fine beginnings of a paleontological museum. We have a long way to go to equal Eastend, and in fact that's probably not going to be a reality or even advisable."

"Yeah, I'm sure the federal and provincial governments won't consider financing another huge research station," said Dad. "However, I think we have a case to fund a research outpost, but that's another topic for some other time."

"Agreed," said Doug Lindstrom.

Pederson shifted in his chair, and added, "Yes, we'll talk about that possibility later. For now, Ed and Doug, are you all set for the weekend's first reservations?"

"Yes, indeed," Dad said.

"We just finished outlining the parking lot this afternoon. Tomorrow we'll haul the garbage cans to the camping sites, and then we can finish the rest area at the dig site," Doug added.

"Fantastic!" Pederson said, and then turned to the ladies. "I probably don't even need to ask, but it wouldn't be fair if I didn't." He looked at them expectantly.

Jed's mom answered for them, "All, A-okay! We'll put the finishing touches on the rest areas and pick up the fresh food we need in town tomorrow."

"All the painting is done, and the kitchen area in the yard is ready to go." Mom nodded confidently. "And it seems you all liked the snacks we're planning on serving," she pointed to the near empty dessert trays.

Everyone laughed.

"No problem there, Libby," Pederson agreed.

"We're ready too," Lucy spoke up from across the table. She handed Cheryl, who'd been sitting in her lap, over to her two younger sisters. They took her to the kitchen to play with her. "I've drawn up the maps for the hiking trails and we've all gone down them a few times."

"Yeah, we put discreet markers in places so no one gets lost." Daniel tried hard not to look over at Jed, but everyone knew who he was talking about anyway, and they all laughed again.

Lucy continued, "I also have the info sheets for the fossil hunters ready to be photocopied."

"Did you make sure the information about it being illegal to take fossils away from the site is in big letters, like Mr. Tokaryk told us to do?" Daniel asked.

Lucy nodded and passed him the sheet.

"Great!" said Pederson. "And I've got the dig sites prepared and roped off, and all the tools ready. Good teamwork everyone!"

They congratulated themselves and the chattering escalated again, until Pederson called them back to attention.

"As you know, the mayor of Climax is bending over backwards to help us, which in turn helps the community by bringing tourists here." Everyone nodded in agreement. "She'd like to see us linked more strongly to the Eastend ventures, including with the RSM. Especially as we're already working with them on the *Edmontosaurus* find."

Everyone nodded and he continued. "We're really starting to attract the tourists to the town now, with the museum up and running. And from the sounds of it, we have quite a number of reservations for camping and day digs out here." He looked at Daniel's mom, who had the reservation book open on the table.

She nodded. "And we're sure to have many who will just drop in without prior notice, which is great too."

Doug said, "Yes, and word has been getting around, so we want to make sure whatever we do here works well. I think we've got a good thing going."

"Guess we'll find out this weekend," Dad said with a wry grin.

"Well, we certainly have a great start," Pederson continued. "When I met with the people at the T.rex Discovery Centre today, they were quite enthusiastic about us becoming partners."

"Yahoo!" Daniel and Jed clapped. "All right!"

"Hold on," Pederson calmed them. "These were just initial talks, and of course we'll have to have many meetings and discussions with their authorities, and with the town council, and so on. As far as they can see, partnering with us will enhance what they are doing as well and it will benefit us all to bring as many people to the area as possible."

"What about the red tape? How many papers are we going to have to sign?" asked Mom.

"Yes, and are they going to have special rules and regulations we're going to have to follow?" Doug asked.

Pederson answered. "Probably all of the above. And of course, we may need to think about extra insurance and other legal costs."

"But it's doable, isn't it?" Daniel asked with sudden concern.

"I'm sure it is, but it can be tedious as all get-out when you start doing the paperwork for government-run operations!"

"Isn't that the truth!" Jed's mom sighed.

"Okay, people, now the hard work of this evening begins. Ed, let's go over your figures first." Pederson pointed to Dad as he shared the graphs with the others. Mom and Greta Lindstrom moved closer to the men at the other end of the table.

Daniel and Jed looked at one another and eased out of their chairs. They weren't interested in the money details. No one seemed to notice them leave. Lucy followed close behind them. Sometimes she annoyed them, but tonight they let her join them as they headed outdoors. They passed by Leanne and Lindsay playing with Cheryl and Dactyl on the back step. Dactyl ignored them. He was getting great attention from all the girls.

The others all seemed to gravitate towards the yard where the kitchen and snack bar were set up. An old tire swing hung from a big tree nearby. Lucy sat twisting on it, while Daniel and Jed sat on some stumps near the firepit a few feet away, chatting idly about the day.

"Those Nelwins sure have some nerve," Jed said. "I'd like to teach them a thing or two."

"Wouldn't we all," said Daniel, pointing to the bruises on his head and face.

"They're such bullies," said Lucy. "Seems they just get away with everything!"

"I've read somewhere that some bullies are actually scared if you stand up to them, but I don't know if that would work with those two. They're so big!"

"Yeah, and they're always together – two picking on one isn't fair!" Lucy added.

"Guess it's best if we just stay out of their way!" Jed said.

"That would be fine, except they keep tracking me." Daniel explained the last couple of days to Lucy. Of course, he left out the bit about going back into prehistoric time.

Restless again, the three of them wandered over the pasture towards the edge of the land before it dipped into the valley. The sun hovered above the horizon in a blaze of oranges and golds. They sat on some rocks and looked over the landscape in front of them. Although it was somewhat scrubby and without monumental landmarks, there was something about the quiet and peacefulness as nighttime neared. A gentle breeze brushed their arms as the crickets started their evening chirpings and the frogs chorused by the dugout.

From where they sat, if they looked to the distant right, they could see the rest station for the hikers, situated halfway down the valley on a flatter area at the top of a hill that gave a panoramic view of the coulee below. A small, open-walled structure, covered with a waterproof roof, had some benches and a couple of picnic tables in it. A hitching post had been erected nearby in case some people chose to ride horses. A couple of empty forty-five-gallon barrels that had years ago contained gas sat by some trees. One was for washing and drinking water for the horses, and one to hold their feed. Another couple of outhouses stood discreetly off to one side.

As Daniel looked, he thought he saw movement, but he couldn't be sure. The fading sun cast a shadow over the site. He ignored it until it happened a second time.

"Do you see something moving down there?" he asked the others.

They fixed their eyes on the rest area, waiting in silence.

"There it is again!" Daniel lowered his voice, afraid to scare whatever it was off before they found out more.

"I saw it," Jed whispered back.

"Me too," Lucy said quietly.

In unison, as if they'd made a verbal agreement, all three of them started moving stealthily down the hillside for a closer look. They darted from rocks to low bushes to dips in the landscape, zigzagging down the hill and keeping as quiet as they could. There was definitely someone down there. They could hear some sort of scraping going on.

"I think there are two of them," Jed whispered from behind a bush.

The closer they got, the lower the sun set, until they were enshrouded in twilight. That made it easier for them to approach unnoticed, but more difficult to see what was going on. There was no mistake, though, when they heard a rough, rowdy laugh, that it was the Nelwin brothers, up to no good.

Sneaking behind the outhouses, they could see the pair sitting on a picnic table, digging at the surface with something. Daniel decided it was time to confront them. They were damaging property! His property! He was just about to come out from hiding when Jed pulled him back.

"They've got a knife!"

Daniel peeked around the corner again. Jed was right! They were using a big jackknife. Probably carving their initials into the table. Daniel gulped and huddled with the others behind the outhouse.

"Now what?" he murmured.

"We get out of here as fast as possible," Jed answered. "We'll let the adults deal with it."

Lucy frantically nodded her head in agreement.

"Okay," Daniel agreed, reluctantly. He motioned for Lucy to go first. He'd take up the rear.

By now it was quite dark and difficult to see where they were going. A moon struggled on the horizon behind them, giving them faint light. They stumbled along, as carefully as they could. Suddenly Lucy tripped.

"Ooof!" she went down with a thud.

"You okay?" Jed asked, as Lucy righted herself quickly. His voice echoed into the night.

"Shhh!" Daniel said behind them.

They all looked towards the Nelwins, who had been alerted by the sound and had stopped their carving. The two talked amongst themselves. Whichever one of them held the knife tucked it away into his pocket, seeming to be alarmed that someone might catch them with it. Then the pair headed towards the sound to investigate.

Daniel, Jed, and Lucy dropped to the ground and lay still. They hoped the Nelwins would give up and go away, as they hadn't ventured very far from the campsite.

"ACHOOO!!" Jed sneezed loudly. Then he whispered, "Sorry."

Daniel touched him on the back, and motioned them all to run. Lucy couldn't see and Daniel had to drop back to grab her.

The Nelwins raced towards them, stumbling over the

clumps of grass. The moon suddenly seemed to shine brighter over the hillside, illuminating them all.

"We know you're out there, Daniel!" Craig shouted.

"We're going to get you now!" Todd taunted them.

"Run hard!" Daniel yelled, making sure Lucy was ahead of him.

As cautiously as he could in the darkness, Daniel ran. When he chanced to look back, he saw the Nelwins weren't far behind them. All of a sudden, Daniel pitched forward. One second he was on his feet and the next he was spitting out dirt. Darn, he hadn't seen the gopher hole! Before he had a chance to recover, the Nelwins reached him. They each grabbed an arm and dragged him to his feet.

"Looky, who we have here!" Todd grinned into his face. "Dino boy!"

Daniel saw Jed and Lucy stop.

"Go!" he yelled at the top of his lungs! "Get help!"

Jed hesitated and started back.

Daniel shouted again. "Take Lucy! Get help!"

Jed grabbed Lucy by the arm and they pelted up the hill as fast as they could go.

Craig made a movement to follow them, but Todd motioned him to stay put.

"Ixnay! Let 'em go. We'll have fun with Dino boy here!" He prodded Daniel forward, dragging him back to the rest area.

"What about the adults coming?" Craig asked, worried.

"Who cares!" Todd said. "By the time they get here, Dino Boy will tell us what we want to know."

"What do you want from me?" Daniel asked, as bravely as he could. He gasped for breath, but Todd had a tight hold on him, and he wasn't about to let go. He could hear the faint sounds of Jed and Lucy pounding up the hillside. Would they be back in time?

"We want to know where your hideout is!" Craig demanded.

"No way!" Daniel said, alarmed. They'd have to torture him to get the information.

"I think we can be convincing," Todd said, poking his angry, pudgy face into Daniel's.

As he spoke, spittle flew onto Daniel's face. He couldn't wipe it off, because they each had one of his arms. He didn't dare say anything to provoke them, as they dragged him along.

"Come on, Craig," Daniel appealed to the brother he knew a little better. "What do you want with my old hideout anyway?"

"We won't know that until we see it, now, will we?" Todd responded with a snarl.

Daniel gulped. How was he going to get away from them without telling?

They held him against the hitching post, while they thought about what they were going to do with him. Daniel's knees felt weak, and his head ached again. His stomach felt a little queasy too! He could hear the faint shouts of Lucy and Jed calling for help as they ran.

"Maybe we should get out of here before anyone comes," suggested Craig, looking up the hillside uneasily.

"Don't wimp out on me now, bro," Todd taunted, not taking his eyes off Daniel.

His eyes lighted on the barrels by the trees. He signalled to Craig.

"What are you going to do?" Craig asked. "There's no time."

"Nothing serious. Just make him talk," Todd said. "Let's take him over there. We'll just have a little fun."

They grabbed Daniel again and hauled him over to the barrels. Todd moved one a little closer to the edge of the hill, while Craig pinned his arms behind his back. Then with only a couple of grunts, they lifted Daniel and stuffed him inside the barrel.

"Hey, what are you doing?" Daniel yelled, kicking and grabbing at them to escape.

"We're not letting you go until you tell us where your hideout is!" Todd breathed into his face.

"I'm not telling!" He defied them again.

"Fine!" Todd pushed him farther into the barrel. "Stay there then!"

Daniel shuddered inside the rusty old barrel. It was hot and confining and all he could do was keep breathing in the dusty metallic air. Every time he tried to push himself upwards, the Nelwins slammed him back down again.

"Just tell us where it is!" Craig had a pleading whine in his voice.

Daniel rested for a few moments, catching his breath. He really was trapped! Maybe if he gave them the wrong directions, they'd go away?

As if reading his thoughts, Todd's words echoed down to him, "Don't even think about telling us a lie!"

"I'm not telling you the truth either!" Daniel spat out at them.

He could hear the two whispering above him, but he couldn't make out the words. From way off in the distance, he thought he heard Dactyl barking. Maybe help was on the way! He just needed to stall.

"Tell us now, Daniel. Time is running out!" Todd hovered above him.

Daniel struck up and punched towards Todd's face. But he was too cramped and didn't connect as well as he'd hoped.

Todd darted back, grabbing his nose.

Daniel heard voices coming down towards them. Yes! Help was on the way!!

"You'll pay for that, Dino boy!"

"Let's just get out of here," Craig implored.

Todd rushed at the barrel and knocked it over. The next thing Daniel felt was his body clashing against metal and he was staring at the ground. Then he felt a force against the barrel and suddenly he was careening down the hillside. He thumped and banged about, yelling as he went. All he could do was protect his face and hands as his body crashed from side to side, and he flopped over with each rotation, banging into the metal walls of the container.

He felt the jolt of every rock and tuft of grass he rolled over. His stomach did flip-flops and his head pounded. There was a terrible clanging in his ears. The horrible tumbling seemed to go on forever, as if time stood still. At one point, he bounced exceptionally hard against a large protrusion and he seemed to be airborne. Then he crashed into some bushes with a resounding clang and came to a shuddering stop.

He lay stunned for a few moments, feeling as if he was still spinning. Every part of his body hurt. He lay there for quite some time, half in and half out of the dented drum, spitting rust. He wiped other flakes of rust out of his face and tried to open his eyes all the way. He could see the stars pinpricking the night sky above him, and when he managed to turn his head, he could see lights bobbing at the top of the hill. He closed his eyes and rested, hoping someone would rescue him soon.

CHAPTER NINE

Dactyl reached Daniel first. He whimpered and padded around Daniel softly, licking his face.

"I'm okay, boy," he said reaching up to pat his side, then dropping his arm back down again, as a pain shot up his arm. He felt so weak.

"He's down this way!" he heard Dad call to the others.

"Daniel!" Mom screamed from farther back.

"I'm okay, Mom," he croaked out.

Just then Dad knelt down by his side, setting his flashlight on the ground so it shone on him, but not in his eyes.

"Son, is anything broken?"

"I don't think so," he murmured. "But I sure do hurt!"

Gently, Dad slid Daniel all the way out of the barrel, and then checked Daniel's arms, his legs, and lastly his neck.

"We'll get you out of here as quick as we can!" Dad rose and called out to Doug, who was just arriving, "We're going to need the truck to lay him in!"

"I'll get it!" Doug answered. "Good thing we left it at the campsite."

He strode off across the pasture and down the next hill, shining a strong beam of light to show the way. From above, Daniel heard Jed's mom shoo the other kids back to the house. He heard her concern over Lucy, and then, when it appeared she was fine, Greta asked her to put the kettle on and take care of Cheryl. Then Daniel felt sure he heard the quick footsteps of his mom, hurrying down the hill.

"Libby, we'll need a warm blanket too," Dad called to Mom. She in turn asked Jed to run back and grab one off the end of the couch.

"I don't think there are any broken bones," Dad added, when Mom reached his side.

"Oh, Daniel!" Mom brushed his hair from his face and kissed his forehead. "You're going to be okay." She examined him for more cuts and bruises, softly checking him again for broken bones.

Moments later, Pederson appeared. "Darn, I lost them!" he said, breathing hard. "At least we have witnesses this time and they won't be able to get away with this! You are going to call the RCMP, aren't you?"

"You bet we will," Mom said without hesitation.

Dad added, "For attacking Daniel and for damaging property too." He'd already heard about them carving the picnic tables from Jed and Lucy.

Jed's mom reached them and stood peering down at

Daniel. He lay dazed on the ground for what seemed like hours, drifting in and out of sleep. Then suddenly there was activity again. Jed arrived, panting, with the blanket. The start of an engine and the grinding of gears told them Doug Lindstrom was on his way uphill with the truck. And Dactyl barked into the night.

After much scuffling of feet and whispering, Daniel felt himself being lifted into the box of the truck. Mom covered him with the blanket and crawled in beside him. Jed and his mom took the front seat, with his dad driving, and Dad, Mr. Pederson, and Dactyl sat on the tailgate. As they bounced back up the hill, Mom tried to keep Daniel as comfortable as possible, but there were still rough spots that jangled his body against the floor of the truck box. He tried to keep from groaning.

Instead, he concentrated on the stars in the sky above. Although they wavered with the movement of the truck, he thought he could pick out the Big Dipper. Doug wove back and forth as he moved up the hill, rather than going straight upwards, so that those in the back of the truck wouldn't have to brace themselves.

When they finally reached home, Dad and Jed's dad carried Daniel into the bright lights of the living room and laid him on the couch. Mom brought out her trusty wash basin and warm water and began wiping the rust flakes and smudges from his face and arms with a soft damp cloth. Daniel gritted his teeth as she applied iodine to disinfect the scrapes. When she finished, she rebandaged his head, and placed a few more bandages where they were needed. Dad phoned the RCMP office in Climax to lay a complaint. Everyone sat quietly in the room, watching Daniel begin to move again. He felt every muscle twinge in pain, and his headache was back in full force.

Dad returned and said, "Constable Fraser was going to come tonight, but I suggested there was no point in rushing out here. It's late, and I figured we all need some rest, especially Daniel. He'll come first thing in the morning."

Jed's mom brought him a glass of water, which was just what he needed. He'd had a dry ride! He looked around at all the concerned faces and was sorry he'd worried everyone. It had been his idea to see what the Nelwins were up to. More of them could have been hurt.

"I always wondered what it would feel like to roll downhill in a barrel," Daniel said, making an attempt at humour. "Now I don't need to wonder anymore!"

Everyone laughed weakly. If he could joke, he was going to be all right! The Lindstroms gathered up their children and offered Pederson a ride home. He accepted with gratitude.

"Take care of yourself, young man!" Pederson said, patting Daniel's hand before he left. "I'll be by tomorrow."

"Okay." Daniel smiled feebly. "Thanks, everyone. Good night!"

Jed lingered behind as the others filed out of the room. He stood by Daniel.

"Talk to you tomorrow, Jedlock!"

"Uh, Daniel, I'm sorry I wasn't more help to you," his friend said, bowing his head and moving closer.

"You did just fine, Jed! You got help. Who knows what else they would have done to me? And you took care of Lucy too."

"Yeah, at least I did that much!" Jed's face brightened a little. "Next time though, I won't leave."

"Let's hope there isn't a next time!" Daniel said wearily.

Jed grinned. "That's for sure. You're pretty beaten up!"

"Don't remind me!" Daniel groaned.

"See ya, buddy!" Jed gave him a light high-five.

Daniel rested while Dad ushered everyone out the back door and safely into the vehicle, and Mom tended to Cheryl. Daniel ached all over! He just wanted to go to bed, and forget the whole incident. He knew more trouble was brewing now! If the police charged the Nelwins, they would try to get him back worse than ever. He knew that there was no reasoning with those two. Look what had happened when he tried to defend himself!

Dad came back with some painkillers and a glass of water, which Daniel swallowed gratefully. While Mom prepared Cheryl for bed, Dad helped Daniel up to his room. Dad left him while he visited the bathroom and changed into his pyjamas. He wobbled about, using the wall and bedposts to steady himself. Every movement hurt. He hoped the painkillers would kick in soon.

Dad tucked the blankets around him, making sure he was cosy. He even brought him a glass of water for on his nightstand. Then he sat at the edge of the bed with a worried look.

"You sure do know how to have an adventure," he said, ruffling Daniel's hair with a soft touch of his hand.

"Guess I do," Daniel agreed. If only Dad knew the half of it!

"At least maybe we can put a stop to the Nelwins hassling you for a time, and who knows, maybe they'll learn a lesson."

"Temporarily, anyway," Daniel added, sighing.

"Yes," Dad agreed, none too happy at the thought. "We'll see what Jim Fraser has to say when you give your statement in the morning."

Daniel nodded. He felt his eyes grow heavy with sleep. The presence of Dad, and the warmth and softness of his bed were comforting. Just before he drifted off to sleep, he suddenly remembered a conversation he'd had with Mr. Pederson earlier in the day.

"Dad," he asked, opening his eyes to look at his father's expression. "Did I put too much pressure on you and Mom about doing this dinosaur tourist thing?"

Dad seemed surprised. "No. Whatever gave you that idea?"

"Well, I just wondered, because I didn't realize until today how much money you might have made if you'd taken the lease offer instead."

"Don't even think it," Dad said. "Remember, the bank suggested we do this instead, because it was more of a sure thing and probably profitable more quickly too."

"Okay, just as long as you're sure."

"I'm sure," Dad said, seeming touched by Daniel's concern.

Daniel yawned and closed his eyes.

A moment later, Mom planted another kiss on his forehead. She must have been standing at the door and stepped over to the bed without either of them noticing.

"Good night, Danny-boy," she whispered.

That was the last thing he heard until morning.

Daniel woke up to Cheryl cooing by his head and poking him in the arm with her chubby fingers.

"Up?" she asked, standing beside him and holding onto her worn teddy bear by its ear.

"I'm up," Daniel said, groaning as he rolled over to face her. His body felt stiff and sore all over. Maybe once he moved around a bit, it would be better.

"Book?" she asked, smiling at Daniel. Her blonde curls lay in disarray all over her head, as if she'd just woken as well.

He sighed. "Okay. Book."

She toddled out of the room and came back carrying her favourite book, *Go Dog Go.*

He reached over and painfully helped Cheryl climb onto his bed. She sat in the middle of the covers in her sleepers. He tried to sit up, but his head pounded, so he lay back down again and helped her crawl up beside him. She lay back on the other pillow, and held the book for him. He began to read just as Mom called in a quiet voice from down the hall.

"Cheryl? Where are you?"

She giggled and her eyes twinkled at Daniel, but she kept silent.

"Cheryl?" Mom called again softly.

"She's here, Mom," Daniel said, and Cheryl tried to hide under the covers.

Mom came to the side of the bed, smiling. She was still in her dressing gown, with her hair all ruffled too.

"Guess Cheryl's gone," said Mom in a singsong voice. "Guess I get to eat her pancakes instead."

All of a sudden, Cheryl threw back the quilt and popped her head out.

"Here!" she said, laughing.

Mom reached over and picked her up, teddy bear, book, and all.

"How are you feeling this morning, son?" she asked, turning her attention to Daniel. She examined his cuts and bruises.

"Stiff, sore," he admitted.

"When you're ready, let's get you up and moving. Getting some circulation going will help," she suggested. "I'll have breakfast on in ten minutes. We all seemed to have slept in this morning."

"Thanks, Mom," Daniel said, glancing at the clock. Nine a.m. They really had slept in. He heard the shower running; must be Dad, running late too.

Then Dactyl began barking below his window and he heard the crunch of gravel as a vehicle drove into the yard. Daniel eased himself out of bed and over to the window. An RCMP vehicle stood in the driveway. He heard Mom hustle down the stairs with Cheryl, then the opening of the back door.

"Good morning, Jim," Mom called out cheerily.

"Morning, Libby," he heard Constable Fraser say.

"Come right in. I'm afraid we're later than usual this morning. We had a rather active late night. I'll get some coffee on right away." He could hear the scrape of a kitchen chair across the linoleum and the squeak as the officer sat down.

"Daniel," Mom called up to him.

"Coming," he called back, reaching for his clothes. Manipulating them and dressing was one of the toughest things he'd done in a long time. This must be what it feels like to be a really old man in pain, he thought, as his body creaked and protested with each movement.

At last he made it downstairs. Dad was already there, shiny and fresh from his shower. The officer had his statement pad out on the table, and Mom poured coffee for everyone, then set a plate of banana muffins down. Cheryl sat in her high chair, mashing a peach. Daniel sat down beside her, suddenly shy with Constable Fraser in their house on police business.

"You know our son, Daniel, from the baseball field, of course," Dad said.

"Sure do!" the constable smiled and shook his hand.

"How are you doing, sir?" Daniel said politely.

"I'd say a mite better than you, by the looks of you, son." He peered over at Daniel with twinkling eyes, taking in all of his wounds and bandages. "Heard you had a bit of a run-in with the Nelwin brothers. They did all of this to you last night?"

"Well, I did have a few marks on my head from something else before that," he admitted, thinking of his encounter with a tree trunk.

"They also ambushed you, and you smashed the back of your head into a rock a couple of days ago," Dad noted.

"Yeah," said Daniel, touching the bandage at the back of his head.

"And tell them what happened on your way to town yesterday," Dad prompted.

Daniel launched into the highway scene and the incident with Lucy. Mom hovered in the background preparing the pancake batter, listening intently. Constable Fraser jotted the important details down on his notepad.

"Guess we can see about adding dangerous driving to

the list of charges. I'll speak to Mr. Pederson and see what he has to say."

He continued to write the account of the night before, without emotion, pausing only to ask for more clarification on some detail as Daniel explained what had happened.

Finally, Constable Fraser stopped writing, tucked the notepad under his arm, and stood up. "Now, I guess I should take a look at the damage from last night."

"Sure thing," Dad said. "We can take the truck."

He turned to Daniel. "Are you up for this, son?"

He nodded and rose out of his chair stiffly. "Just a little sore, is all," he said, limping to the door.

When they arrived at the rest area, they found only one picnic table had been seriously damaged with carvings. But the Nelwins had spray-painted the backs of the outhouses in glowing purple and orange offensive graffiti. They also saw evidence of various objects having been shifted. The garbage cans were tipped over and one of the benches parked upside down over the hitching post.

Daniel stood at the edge of the hill and looked down to where the barrel lay damaged at the bottom, resting beside some bushes.

Beside him, Constable Fraser whistled. "That's quite a hill."

The hill was even steeper and longer than Daniel recalled. No wonder the horrible trip down had taken so long! The constable started heading down.

"Hop in the truck," Dad offered. "We'll go down the easy way."

Reluctantly, Daniel climbed in. He wasn't eager to see that barrel again. As they jostled along, a warm breeze puffed into the open windows. Songbirds greeted them, and a few grasshoppers made their first morning forages. The sun was already warm and the few clouds drifted high in the sky. It was going to be another hot day!

The offending barrel, although dented from the unexpected trip down the hillside, would still be useful as a container for grain or water. Once Constable Fraser had a look at where it lay, Dad tipped it back upright. Daniel peered inside. The interior was covered with rust flakes, most of which had fallen off on the tumble down. Dad turned it over and banged out the loose grit. Then he loaded it onto the back of the truck.

"You certainly do have a lively anecdote to tell now," said Constable Fraser. "Good thing you weren't more seriously hurt!"

"I know," said Daniel.

They slowly made their way back up to the rest area in the truck. Once the barrel had been deposited in its place, they headed for the house. They stood talking in the yard by the police car.

"So what happens now?" Daniel asked, dreading the outcome.

"Well, I'll go and have a little chat with Jed and Lucy, then with the Nelwins."

"Then what?"

"We'll see if the story checks out –"

Daniel started to protest. The constable held up his hand, motioning him to wait to hear everything he had to say, and continued.

"Which it probably will, seeing as how you have two witnesses."

"So they'll be out of the way for a while?" Dad asked.

The Constable pursed his lips. "Well, it depends on what you want to do. The process could take some time. They could be charged, if we feel the mischief and bodily harm warrant it," he automatically put up his hand again to stop Daniel from protesting, "then they'll go to court in Shaunavon. If they plead guilty, the judge will decide on the sentencing, but if they plead not guilty and it goes to trial, the process could take several months."

Daniel sighed and shook his head, then looked up at his dad, who didn't seem too happy about the prospect either.

"Well, at least then they'll be put away for a while, right?" Daniel asked with renewed enthusiasm.

"Not necessarily. Only if they're convicted and if they have several previous serious offences, then the judge might sentence them to some time in a juvenile detention centre," the constable said. "That could take a while. And they probably won't be held in custody while they await trial."

"So then, what are the possibilities for punishment?" Dad asked. "Or even of restitution?"

"Depends on how lenient the judge is and how serious he feels the other charges against them were in the past. These two are fairly well-known in these parts," the constable answered. "This is a case of assault and we can certainly charge them, if all the conditions are met in the investigation. The judge might give them one last chance and tell them that with the next offence they'll go to jail, or a youth facility. Then he might sentence them to restitution and/or community service, and probably some counselling.

"But they'll be back at it again soon either way, won't they?" Daniel asked.

"That's always a possibility."

Daniel looked over at Dad for support and asked, "So what good is charging them going to do?"

"Let's hope they can't keep doing these kinds of things without some sort of serious consequences," Dad said, clearly agitated by the possibility that the Nelwins might not have to suffer what he thought were proper consequences for their actions.

"At least, they'll have to consider what they've done," said Constable Fraser, "and counselling sometimes helps."

Dad stroked his chin thoughtfully, and his eyes seemed deep in thought.

Daniel sighed. They'd also have time to think about how to get back at him when they were free again.

"What do you want done, then?" the constable asked.

Daniel could see no great long-term solution, only

maybe a reprieve for a bit, if the Nelwins stayed clear of him while their charges were pending.

“”Restitution would be good for a start,” Dad said, surveying the damage. “I don’t know that locking them up would help anything. It never did their father any good! What do you think, Daniel?”

“Yeah. They sure made a mess!” Daniel agreed, shaking his head. “A lot of hard work gone down the tubes.”

Constable Fraser said, “All right, I’ll get this paper-work filed and go talk to the others involved. I happen to know the Nelwins aren’t going very far. I’ve confiscated their dad’s truck. He was a little unstable for driving last night. The boys will be sticking close to home.”

Somehow that didn’t feel very reassuring to Daniel.

CHAPTER TEN

Dad came out to help Daniel with the chores, and by the time they were finished, he found Mom had been right. He didn't seem quite so sore. Not that he could do any acrobatic movements or run any marathons, but at least he could function again without being in total pain.

Just as they finished a hearty breakfast of pancakes and eggs, Mr. Pederson arrived to check on Daniel. He sat down for a cup of coffee.

"Glad to see you're none the worse for wear, young man," Pederson said. "I don't suppose you feel like coming over to the dig site for a while this morning?"

"You bet I do," Daniel looked over at Mom for approval. He might be in pain, but he didn't want to miss an opportunity to do some digging.

She nodded reluctantly.

"Just as long as you stay out of the sun as much as possible, and if you're tired or feel sick, you come home right away."

He nodded and turned to Dad.

"Dad, can you spare me?"

"You bet. Doug and I are almost done the other work at the campsite. Besides, the work you're doing is important too!"

Daniel was pleased to hear his dad so enthusiastic.

"When do you want me?" Daniel asked Mr. Pederson.

"Any time you're ready."

"How about now?"

Pederson pushed his chair back and got up. "Okay."

Daniel suddenly remembered that Jed was probably coming over with his dad. "Is it okay if Jed comes later?"

"Certainly! We'll make a paleontologist out of him yet!"

Everyone laughed. Jed was forever getting things mixed up.

"We'll send him to the dig," said Dad before Daniel could ask.

"But he may get lost," Daniel said, suddenly worried about his friend's problem with directions.

"I'll make sure he gets there." Dad smiled.

Just then the phone rang. Mom answered it.

"Just a moment, please. He happens to be right here." She motioned to Pederson. "It's the RSM in Regina, some news about your *Edmontosaurus*, Roxanne."

As Pederson listened, his eyes became excited. "Yes, thank you, it's good to have confirmation. Sure thing. Thanks. I appreciate your calling."

He hung up the phone and turned to the others in the room. "They think they may know how our *Edmontosaurus* died. They've been preparing the left hind quarter and found some breakage in the bones." He turned to Daniel. "They're e-mailing some photos to your computer later today."

"Wow!" Daniel said, pleased that progress was being made on finding out about Roxanne's life.

"This is exciting!" Mom went to hug Daniel, but seeming fearful of hurting him, held back, smiling at him. Dad gave him a thumbs-up.

"Let's go, Daniel!" Pederson said with a spry step towards the door. "Time to see what we can find today!"

Daniel hurried to grab his backpack, water, and tools. Mom sent a thermos of coffee along for Mr. Pederson and a few cookies for the both of them for a mid-morning snack.

"Will you be back for lunch?" she asked, "or should we bring it out to you?"

"Ahh," Pederson looked tempted, but reluctant to put anyone to extra trouble.

"Never mind," said Mom with a laugh. "I know how you two get caught up in what you're doing. I'll make sure something gets out to you."

"Much obliged, ma'am," Pederson said with a grin of relief on his face.

"You're the greatest, Mom!" Daniel added and gave her a quick hug. He meant it in several ways. She didn't fuss over him as much as some moms did, and she had some good ideas sometimes. What he liked best was that she really listened to him when he talked to her.

Once outside, Pederson picked up the gear he'd left on the back step and they headed across the farmyard in the general direction of Daniel's hideout. It was also the way to Pederson's home and to the new dig site. Dactyl trotted along beside them. They were careful to make sure no one was following or otherwise spying on them. Daniel still didn't trust the Nelwins. The police probably hadn't talked to them yet. However, they reached the site without incident.

As they dropped down a hill into the fossil quarry site, the sun was high in the morning sky, casting shadows across the immediate south side of the slope. A portion of the dig had been roped off where Pederson was doing his serious work. He didn't want anyone touching it, except maybe Daniel. The rest of the dig was portioned off in sections where the tourists could try their hands at fossil finding. The sections were cut into the hillside at various levels of rock formations. A crude path ran along the top of Pederson's special area so that those on tour could watch him work. He would also take time to explain to them what he was doing.

For now the two unwrapped their tools and set to work on an area covered with a light tarp to keep the rain off. Not that there had been any rain for several weeks, but they weren't taking any chances. So far they weren't sure what the exposed, dark brown-pitted bones belonged to, but they hoped to uncover enough by the end of the day to determine if they were part of a large skeleton or a smaller animal of some kind.

Carefully, they descended the rugged side of the hill into the pit, making sure they didn't dislodge any rocks or stones. On their hands and knees, they lifted the tarp and folded it, setting it to the side. A hawk sailed high overhead in the clear sky. The chattering of swallows and the clear *caw-caw-caw* of a crow sounded across the valley.

While Daniel worked on one end, Pederson took the other. Dactyl sniffed around the site for a bit, but mostly seemed bored with the lack of attention and soon wandered off back home. He'd already experienced all-day digs and never stayed long. The occasional garden-variety snake or sand lizard that showed up didn't interest him much. He preferred searching for the sharp-tailed grouse or grey partridge that inhabited the area.

First Daniel used a narrow brush to disperse the dirt from a small area, and then he used a small curved pick to clean debris out of a crevice. After several minutes, he pushed his cap back from his forehead and studied the round piece he'd uncovered. It looked like the tip of some kind of tooth. He continued, oblivious to Pederson working in silence across from him.

The sun rose higher and the day became hotter, but it wasn't until Pederson tapped him on the shoulder that Daniel even thought about stopping for a drink of water.

"Let's not get dehydrated," he said, passing him the water flask.

They took a break then, sitting against the hillside in the only spot of shade they could find. As they munched on Mom's chocolate chip cookies, they surveyed their work.

"I think I might have found a small tooth." Daniel explained what he'd done so far.

Pederson said, "I'll come and take a look at it, and you might want to see what I've found."

Daniel noticed the catch in Pederson's voice and looked at him in surprise. He had a twinkle in his eyes again, which meant he'd discovered something really interesting. They crouched down at Daniel's spot first.

"Yes," said Pederson, peering at the exposed piece with his magnifying glass. "I'd say it's definitely a tooth. Looks like it's more rounded, maybe from a herbivore."

Pederson sat back on his heels with his hands on his knees. "Good work, my boy! Now let's take a look at my portion."

They climbed over to the other side of the fossil cavity. Daniel studied the shape and felt along the curve of the rough, narrow bone.

"Is it a rib?" Daniel asked, puzzled by the thinness.

"I think so, but not of a dinosaur. At least not unless it's a very young one, but I don't think so." His voice held a touch of excitement.

"What *do* you think it is?" Daniel asked, not able to keep his curiosity from showing.

"Keep it to yourself, now!" Pederson reminded him.

Exasperated, Daniel promised. "Have I ever told before?"

"No, but it can't hurt to remind you!" Pederson smiled. Then he took a breath and said, "It may be a flying reptile!"

"Cool!" Daniel knew how rare it was to find them. Generally, their skeletons were so delicate that they rarely withstood the ravages of so much passing time. They usually disintegrated from being transported down a river, where the bones crumbled along the stream or riverbed, and then from various erosional factors, such as wind, rain, or snow in the current world.

Pederson examined the rib through his magnifier, then picked up a little brush and began working again. He seemed to forget all about Daniel standing beside him. Daniel moved away quietly and went back to his workplace.

Maybe an hour later, they heard a repetitious scuffling, plodding sound and looked up at each other.

"Jed!" they said in unison. He always made a great deal of noise, so you could tell when he was around.

Moments later, his blond curls appeared over the hilltop. Besides his backpack, he carried a small cooler. Mom had found a way to send lunch!

"Hi, guys! I'm here at last," he said, plopping the cooler onto the ground, and sliding it down the hill to the walkway above them.

Daniel ran to catch it to make sure it didn't tumble into the trench. Jed made his way down the uneven path to the their work site.

"Finding anything interesting?" asked Jed curiously, peering into the pit.

Pederson gave Daniel a warning glance.

"It's always interesting," said Daniel. "I'm working on a small tooth and Mr. Pederson has a rib or something over there."

"Great!" Jed said. "What would you like me to do first?"

Pederson stood up. "How about in this area here?"

Pederson walked over to a slightly lower level from where he and Daniel worked. This area needed to be cleared before they could start the more delicate, detailed work. It was also one they wanted the visitors to be able to experiment with.

"I'll get you some tools." Pederson handed Jed a small shovel and a brush.

"I'll be careful," Jed said, anticipating a lecture from Pederson.

Jed chattered non-stop as he worked, asking Daniel what had happened since the night before. Daniel filled him in on the police investigation. Then Jed told him about the questions they'd asked Lucy and him.

"Good thing we were there to back you up this time!" Jed said.

"Yeah, maybe now they'll be able to stop them hassling people."

Jed stood up in sudden realization. "But, yikes, they'll really be after you now that you turned them in!"

"I know," Daniel said, wishing he'd never laid eyes on them in his whole life. "Maybe I'll have to move," he said, half-joking. The other half of him was seriously considering it.

As he stood there, he took off his cap and wiped the sweat and dust from his forehead. The sun was right at high noon, and his stomach said it was time for lunch. He headed towards the food cooler, motioning to the others along the way. Pederson grunted and picked a little more at something. Then he joined the boys on the walkway, where they sat with their feet dangling over the edge.

As they chomped down the fresh ham and cheese with garden lettuce sandwiches Mom had packed for them, they stared at the panoramic vista of sharp hills within the steep valley. There was a lot of land to search for fossils.

"Boggles the mind, doesn't it?" Pederson said aloud, expressing how they all felt.

Daniel handed out the boxes of juice and some carrot sticks, saving the yummy-looking chocolate cake for last. He noticed Mom had also sent extra bottles of water, and some granola bars for later.

After lunch they set back to work in earnest. But before they went back to their special spots, Pederson had them make sure everything was ready for the weekend's first visitors. Then he had each of them practise their tour guide spiel until he was confident they could carry it through without any hesitations.

"Great work, boys," Pederson praised them. "We'll have Lucy go through it first thing tomorrow. Now, anyone have any questions before we get back to digging?"

"No, sir," Jed said, picking up his shovel.

Daniel shook his head. "Nor me. Time to get back to the fun work." He stepped carefully back over to his place. Focused on his work again, he was hardly aware of all the pain niggling throughout his body.

Daniel and Jed quit work about three, satisfied that they'd done as much as they could for the day in preparation for the weekend. Pederson preferred to stay behind and work on his pet project.

"Before you go, though, let's take a look at the work we accomplished today."

Daniel and Jed joined Pederson and could see several more uncovered ribs. Pederson didn't do any explaining. Then they moved on to Daniel's teeth. He'd exposed several more in a curved row. All of them were fairly small. When they reached Jed's area, he shuffled uneasily.

"I sort of thought this might be something," he said, pointing to some strange scratchy markings he'd brushed clear of debris. "But I guess it's only my imagination."

"What did you think it was, lad?" Pederson questioned him closely.

"Some kind of footprints, like bird prints or something, but that couldn't be right, could it?" Jed's face flushed with embarrassment.

"Why not?" Pederson asked.

Jed shrugged his shoulders. "I don't know enough about paleontology," he said.

Daniel bent to take a closer look. There was something peculiar about the markings and about the way Pederson queried Jed. He opened his eyes wide in surprise. They were birdlike prints! Daniel was about to agree with Jed, when Pederson motioned him to be silent.

"Show me them." Pederson suggested.

Jed got down on his hands and knees and began pointing out the markings; where they began and where they ended, as far as he'd cleared the ground. As he moved along, he gained more confidence.

"Tell me what made you think they might be prints." Pederson eyed him in all seriousness.

Jed studied them and thought about the question. "Well, they seem to go in a consistent pattern, for one thing."

"Good," Pederson said, encouraging him to continue. "What else?"

"I guess they reminded me of chicken prints in the mud. But that puzzled me too, because they seem too tiny."

"Very good, Jed!" Pederson clapped him on the back. "You've got it right. They are small, but there were birdlike creatures that size, and they certainly are consistent."

"Do you know what made them?" Jed asked, keenly interested.

"Not yet, but we'll keep working on them to see if we can figure them out. This could be quite a rare find!"

"All right!" said Jed, excited that he'd found something so unusual. "Wait until I tell everyone!"

"Whoa, now, Jed. Hang on a moment," Pederson calmed him down. "That's my first rule of paleontology. You keep things to yourself until you know a little more about them." He gave Jed a stern look. "Do you think you can do that, at least for a couple of days?"

Jed squirmed with his conscience. "I can sure promise to try!"

"Okay," said Pederson, raising his eyebrows. He seemed to know that was the best Jed could do.

"I'll be back first thing tomorrow!" Jed said, gathering up his tools and laying them in an orderly fashion beside his station.

"Daniel, how about we rope this section off now, and keep it especially for Jed?"

Daniel nodded in agreement. "You bet!" He knew what an honour it was for Jed to be singled out and acknowledged in this way.

They accomplished the task in short order and prepared to leave Pederson to his work. Daniel made sure the site was clean from their lunch, and tucked his tools under the tarp. Then he loaded his rock hammer and other belongings into his backpack and put it on.

"You sure you don't want to come back with us?" Daniel asked, a little concerned about the old man being left on his own.

"I'll be fine here," Pederson said, digging out his camera. He was going to record the day's work. "But I'll see you first thing in the morning right back here!"

"You bet," Jed said, clambering out of the quarry in a flurry of excitement.

"Sure will," Daniel said, certain that Pederson would have a special piece of information to show them by then.

Daniel grabbed the food cooler and followed Jed. The container felt light now, but he wondered how Jed had carried it so far.

"Your dad carried it to that hill over there." Jed pointed to the closest one several hundred metres away. "He made sure I knew where to find you!"

Daniel laughed.

"Can you believe it?" Jed asked, his voice up several notches. "I actually found something good!"

"Great work, Jedlock!" Daniel shook his friend's hand. "Now you're a bona fide paleontologist."

"I never knew how exciting it could be," Jed said, his eyes glowing with pleasure. "Do you think we could look at some of your books and see if we can figure out what it might be?"

"Sure can!" Daniel said, pleased with his friend's sudden enthusiasm.

They followed a little gully and then headed up

another hillside. Just as they reached the top, Daniel grabbed Jed's arm.

"Look, over there!" He pointed towards the left where two figures walked furtively over the crest of a hill and disappeared. "I'd swear that was the Nelwins! I thought they would have been arrested or something by now."

Jed stood beside him, worried. "Let's not go looking for trouble," he said, pulling Daniel in another direction.

"But they're headed in the direction of my hideout!" Daniel shrugged Jed's hand off his arm. "I can't let them find it. Who knows what they'll destroy!"

Daniel dropped the cooler and started running.

CHAPTER ELEVEN

Daniel heard Jed panting behind him as he tried to keep pace, but Daniel didn't slow down at all. He had to reach his hideout before the Nelwins! His backpack felt heavy and slapped his back as he ran, but he couldn't take time to remove it. By the time he reached the peak of the hill, his head pounded and he ached all over again. But he couldn't stop!

"Wait, Daniel," Jed pleaded from several yards behind him. "You can't take them on yourself!"

Ignoring Jed, Daniel raced on, stumbling over hillocks of grass and avoiding gopher holes and cacti. He wove down the grassy hill swiftly, almost close to falling several times. His lungs ached with each breath he took, but still he forged ahead. The scent of sage wafted into his nostrils as he ran.

Over the next rise, he stopped for a moment, bending over with his hands on his knees, breathing hard while he surveyed the scene below. The two figures rummaging around were definitely the Nelwins! And they were almost at his hideout!

Taking in big gulps of air, he ran forward. He wasn't sure what he'd do when he got to them, but he couldn't let them inside! They were using big sticks to poke into piles of branches and into holes in the ground. Only a few more yards and they'd be at the base of the two hills where his hideout lay! And then it would only be a few minutes before they'd discover the entrance!

He could hear the rhythmic thud of his footsteps in his ears, which might mean the Nelwins would notice him too, if he got much closer. He spotted a small clump of bushes and dived into them. Catching his breath, he plotted the best way down without being seen. Jed arrived and flopped onto the ground beside him.

"I didn't know you could move so fast!" Jed wheezed. "Now what?"

"That's what I'm trying to figure out." Daniel studied the coulee. "I think we can zigzag our way down." He pointed out the low spots and some bushes and outcroppings where they might go unseen until they could surprise them. "If they see us first, though, we're dinosaur grub!"

Stealthily, Daniel and Jed made their way down the slope one at a time, crouching behind whatever cover they could find. The Nelwins were busy poking and prodding around the hideout and didn't hear their quiet approach.

"Hey, look at this!" Craig yanked at a branch. "I think there's something here!"

Excitedly, the two threw down their poking sticks. In quick, easy movements, they pulled branches and debris out of the way, throwing them aside into a random pile. Moments later, they'd revealed the entrance. Daniel beckoned Jed to hurry as he neared the bushes by the cave.

"Yahoo! Dino boy can't stop us now!" Todd shouted. The two dropped to the ground and crawled inside.

"Just what do you think you're doing?" yelled Daniel behind them.

"Oooh! Dino boy's here!" Craig taunted him from inside the hideout. "We're scared now."

"Get out of there!" Jed hollered beside Daniel.

"Oh, great," said Craig sarcastically, "Dino boy's nerd friend is here too."

"Oooh. We're shaking in our boots!" Todd mocked them from the doorway.

They could hear some shuffling going on. Obviously, the Nelwins were pawing through his belongings.

"Come out of there!" Daniel demanded, worried about what they'd wreck.

"Yeah, come out and face us!" Jed added, looking over at Daniel with fear on his face. He mouthed, "Now what do we do?"

Daniel looked around for something to defend himself with. He pulled a couple of branches off the pile by the doorway and handed one to Jed. They positioned themselves ready for battle at the entrance. Neither one of them was a scrapper, nor did they have an inkling about how they were going to defend themselves. Daniel felt his chest tighten. He gripped the branch tighter and took a warrior stance like one he'd seen in the *Terminator* movies.

"Come out now!" Daniel ordered, feeling anger rise from the pit of his stomach.

Laughter radiated from inside the hideout.

The Nelwins found them amusing! Daniel gritted his teeth, and yelled, "This is your last chance!"

More laughter!

"Come and get us," guffawed Todd weakly, bursting into more laughter.

"Whoa, look at this!" Craig said to his brother. "Weird markings on these ones. Let me see your knife, Todd. Maybe I can add a few more scratches on them."

That did it! Daniel dropped the branch without thinking clearly and charged inside. Craig sat on the stump in the middle of the cave, clawing through Daniel's fossil rocks. Todd kicked at the belongings along the wall.

"What a pile of useless junk!" Todd picked up a snakeskin. When he saw Daniel, he snapped it in two.

Daniel felt a sharp spurt of anger. He attacked Todd barehanded. But the older brother threw him off as if he were a small, bothersome bug. Daniel scraped his knees against the stones Craig had dumped on the ground. Daniel quickly dusted himself off as best he could. He felt the stinging cuts on his hands and knees. As he clenched his hands, preparing to attack, he noticed Jed poking his head inside, letting his eyes adjust to the light.

Craig sniggered. "Bonus! Dino boy and his moron sidekick are going to take us on!"

Jed rushed to Daniel's side. "Why don't you just leave!" he suggested more defiantly than he felt. "You've done enough damage!"

"Not finished yet!" Todd snarled, kicking stones at Daniel and Jed.

"Yeah, " said Craig belligerently. "We still have a few more things to look at." He bent to tip over another pail of stones. "Not that there's anything worthwhile here!"

"Get off my property now!" Daniel demanded through clenched teeth, staring fiercely at the Nelwins.

Jed stood up taller beside Daniel and took a deep breath in preparation for a fight.

Neither of the Nelwins budged.

"Please just leave, before someone gets hurt again!" Jed implored the Nelwins.

"It's payback time!" Todd said, challenging them.

Then Craig pinned Daniel to the wall, while Todd viciously knocked over Daniel's pile of bones, tore pages out of his research book, and ripped at his stashes of snacks, pocketing them. He spied the collection of arrowheads.

"Maybe these are worth something?" Todd said, grabbing the arrowheads and stuffing them into his pockets.

As if watching everything in slow motion, Daniel thought about how lucky he was that his tools were still at the site. They probably would have stolen them, too, if they figured they were of value.

As Daniel struggled against Craig, Jed jumped at Craig and grabbed at his arms, hoping to release Daniel. Out of the corner of his eye, Daniel could see Todd stomping on his bird's nest.

"That'll teach you to get us into trouble!" Todd sneered at him, as he tossed other belongings around the cave.

"Yeah," Craig added, bashing at Jed, who went flying. "Like we need the cops on our case!" He released Daniel abruptly and stepped aside.

"This is just the beginning!" The two brothers surveyed the scene, happy with the mess they'd strewn about the place.

Daniel stood rooted one moment, looking in horror at the chaos, while everyone attempted to catch their breath.

For a split second it was as if time froze.

An instant later, Daniel snapped! He rushed at the Nelwins, grabbing Todd's arm to swing him around towards the entrance.

Jed closed in on Craig, but was grabbed again by Craig's beefy arms and flung against the cave wall. He let out a loud *whoof* of air and sat dazed on the floor for a few seconds. Meanwhile, Daniel struggled with Todd, who flung him aside like a chunk of driftwood.

Suddenly, Daniel remembered the piece of bark under the pot lid, just as Craig Nelwin reached for it.

"What's this?" Craig lifted the lid.

"No!!" screamed Daniel, flying at Craig to push him aside. At that exact moment, Todd grabbed at Daniel's arm. They all connected just as Craig picked up the chunk of bark.

A sharp sizzling sound rent the air, along with Jed's piercing scream.

SPLASH!

Daniel, Craig, and Todd landed in a shallow, muddy pool of water. Craig sat on the bottom, clutching the bark, totally speechless, with his mouth hanging open. Todd still clung to Daniel's arm, gaping in disbelief at a heavily armoured *Ankylosaurus,* pawing the moist ground with its hooves only a few feet in front of them. A pterosaur-like creature screeched overhead.

Daniel recovered first, realizing they'd all been transported back into prehistoric time. A half second later, he remembered about the piece of bark and sprang to snatch it from Craig's hand. But Todd still held his arm and instinctively tightened his grip when Daniel moved. Or maybe he clung in reaction to sheer terror!

As Daniel tried to shake free, Todd made a low, guttural sound and turned to stare at Daniel, his eyes wide in shock. With a forceful jerk, Daniel freed himself and scrambled to his feet. He yanked at Craig's arm.

"Get up, both of you! Now! MOVE!" Daniel screamed at them. He'd just caught sight of what he thought might be a *Troodon,* coming down a path through the trees some distance away. Although a

Troodon was human-sized and small in comparison to other dinosaurs, it was one of the smartest and fastest of the meat-eaters. And one of the most vicious!

Daniel yanked both of them to their feet amid a flurry of splashing water and mud. He'd also noticed what looked like a long, rough, greenish log a few metres away, turning slowly in their direction. Probably a *Borealosuchus*-type crocodile, but he didn't want to find out for sure! And he didn't want to scare the still speechless Nelwins any more than they already were.

They slogged through the muddy sea bottom through the reeds and cattails. When they reached the shore and Daniel tried to make the Nelwins pass the tanklike *Ankylosaurus,* they balked.

Huge horns projected from the back of its head and large oval plates similar to medieval armour scaled its leathery skin, except for two rows of spikes along its back. The most dangerous part looked to be the powerful club-like tail. One flick and they'd all be ancient history too!

"We'll be eaten alive!" Craig whimpered, falling back behind Todd.

"No! It's a herbivore!" Daniel urged them forward. "It eats plants!" he yelled when they didn't move. "Come on, we have to get to safety, FAST!"

The *Ankylosaurus* looked up as they passed, but otherwise paid them no attention, continuing to dig at tuberous roots of some kind. Daniel peered about as they headed for the trees in the opposite direction from where he'd spotted the *Troodon.* Maybe the *Troodon* would be sidetracked by the *Ankylosaurus,* although it would have a hard time penetrating through the tough bony plates that protected the herbivore.

Daniel herded the Nelwins along, keeping them hidden as much as he could by the cycads and other bushes as they made their way over to the tall redwoods. Could they climb a tree? He hoped so. They gawked about in stunned awe, plodding and stumbling along, their muddy pant legs and runners soaked. They didn't seem to be able to take in what was going on.

"Where is this place?" Todd whispered, as a huge dragonfly droned past him. He stared at it, slipping on some thick moss underfoot and startling a small rodent-like animal. Probably a *Purgatorius,* Daniel thought, having brushed up on the Cretaceous Period intently over the last couple of days.

"Prehistoric time – the Cretaceous Period to be exact!" Daniel informed him, jabbing a finger into Craig's back. "Thanks to your bone-headed brother."

"What'd I do?" Craig asked, astounded and offended. He still held the piece of bark.

Daniel wasn't sure what to do about the bark. He figured if they let it go, they'd go back into their current life, but besides needing to convince them of the need to drop it, they probably all had to be touching for it to work, so that someone wasn't left behind. He hoped it wasn't him! First, he had to make them understand what was going on.

"That!" Daniel pointed to the bark.

"This? It's just a dumb piece off a tree," Craig said with disdain, opening his palm where the chunk lay.

"It's not just any 'dumb piece,'" Daniel declared. "It's the reason we're here! Don't drop it! Better yet, how about giving it to me?"

"No way!" Craig said, clenching the bark inside his fist.

"See those giant trees over there?" Daniel pointed. "Now look at the piece of bark."

All three of them stared as if mesmerized.

"You don't see that kind of tree back home, do you?" asked Daniel, as he dragged them under a cycad while they discussed the situation.

"I guess not," Craig answered, crouching tight beside his brother.

"But how did you get it?" Todd asked, as Daniel pulled at his legs so they weren't sticking out.

Daniel sighed. "That's a long story, I'll tell you sometime. Trust me, it's why we're here. So how about handing it back to me and we'll go home now?"

"No way!" Todd said, suddenly. "You're making this all up. You just want that piece of bark because it's valuable. You used some sort of visual projection thing to make us think we're in dinosaur time. We've had enough! Turn off your wacky DVD machine or whatever it is and let's go home."

Daniel stared at Todd in disbelief. Why wouldn't he believe where he was? How much more proof could he possibly want?

"How would I be able to do that?" Daniel asked, astounded. "Where would the power come from?"

"You and that old bone hunter probably cooked something up between you!" Craig defended his brother. "You two are weird!"

"Is that so?" Daniel said, pointing at the ground beside Todd. "Well, then I dare you to touch that snake coming your way."

Todd leapt out of the ferns. Obviously, real or not, snakes terrified him. Daniel and Craig followed Todd. The creature with its menacing-looking head, beady eyes, and long fat body slithered past them in a rustling of underbrush. If the reptile hadn't been so scary, Daniel would have laughed at the look on Todd's face. But they had other terrors to handle. Straight ahead was the back end of something larger than a school bus!

Daniel motioned them to a stop and mouthed to them to be quiet. Slowly, he dropped to his knees and crawled towards some bushes as quietly as he could. He inspected it for inhabitants, then seeing it was safe, motioned the others to follow. They crowded under the branches of several white flowering bushes, perhaps small magnolias.

He whispered to them, "I don't know what kind of dinosaur it is yet. I can't see enough of it, but we'll assume it's dangerous." He pointed to the redwoods several yards away on the other side of the bushes. "That's where we need to go."

He stared hard at Craig. "How about giving me the bark now?"

Craig shook his head defiantly.

"Well, then, at least put it in your pocket, so you don't drop it or lose it!" Daniel commanded. There wasn't any time to argue!

When the bark was safely stowed in Craig's jeans pocket, Daniel motioned them to follow. He led them through the underbrush on their hands and knees. They swatted at strange flying insects and kicked away several crawling things on the ground. Although they'd existed in a cocoonlike space while in the bushes, a cacophony of sounds whirled all around them.

From his previous experiences, Daniel could pick out the loud screeching of the pterosaurs, which flew overhead in the direction of the water. The droning of insects and snuffling of small mammals in the forest cascaded around them. And the earth seemed to tremor from time to time as some large creature plodded over the terrain. With any luck it wasn't a *T. rex*!

Reaching the outside edge of the bushes, Daniel looked around. The redwoods were several hundred metres away across an open, marshy meadow. They also had to find a way across the narrow riverbed. He hadn't seen it when they'd started out. He felt little doubt that he'd returned to the same time and place, although he didn't understand how that had happened.

They plunged forward, carefully making their way

through the tall grasses and down to the riverbank. They followed the river's meanderings along the edge, looking for a shallow place to cross. Several hundred metres ahead, Daniel saw a curve and a likely looking place. As they plodded along, they kept watch all around them. Daniel assigned Todd the ground, Craig the water, and himself the sky and the top of the riverbank. Secretly, though, he watched for any kind of movement anywhere. They were too out in the open and could easily be attacked at any moment.

As they rounded the curve, Daniel heard some sort of snorting sound. He stopped in his tracks and motioned the others to stay still. As he crept forward, the noise became louder and he thought he heard a little squeak. Slowly he moved closer to the bend. His heart pounded as he peered around a piece of protruding earth.

In amazement he stared at the bulky body of an *Edmontosaurus* lying on its side curled by a huge nest. She lay underneath an embankment of earth several yards high that had once been carved out by a raging river. It hung precariously over the nest where some of the eggs were cracked as if the babies were going to hatch.

Daniel inched closer. The mother's huge left hind-quarter seemed bent at a peculiar angle. Her sides heaved and her breathing came in short snorts. Her eyes were closed and she seemed oblivious to his approach or to her hatching babies. She let out another moaning snort. She was hurt! Was she the *Edmontosaurus* from the first time he'd been transported into prehistoric time?

Daniel trembled in excitement! The *T. rex* must have injured her before he attacked the *Stegoceras.* Was there anything he could do for her? She didn't seem able to move. And she was huge!

Before he had time to think of anything, Craig called shrilly, "Daniel, hurry!" Backing away from the *Edmontosaurus* and her nest, Daniel headed back to the Nelwin brothers.

"What took you so long?" Todd demanded.

"An injured *Edmontosaurus,*" Daniel answered, peering around for danger.

"Todd thought you'd left us!" Craig declared. Todd stomped on his brother's foot to keep him quiet.

Out of the corner of his eye, Daniel saw a flying reptile circling farther down the river. Time to get moving to safety! That's when he noticed some kind of huge dinosaur he'd never heard about before, standing in the middle of the river a few yards downstream. It stood about fifteen feet high with a long neck, munching on water plants. Daniel could see most of its legs. The river wasn't that deep. They could probably walk across it!

Choosing a narrow point nearby, Daniel waded into the water, keeping a sharp lookout for crocodiles and other dangerous water creatures. Looking down, he noted that he could see his feet, and the water was clear all the way across. Good thing, because he wasn't much of a swimmer, and didn't relish going for a dip in the unknown river.

He motioned the Nelwins forward, and they crossed as swiftly as they could. Craig and Todd seemed to know that silence was best and they kept the ripples to a minimum so as not to attract predators. Daniel tried not to think about anything that might be lurking in the water. The sandy bottom sucked at their sneakers each time they took a step, but once they'd started, they didn't stop until they reached the opposite side.

Daniel sighed in relief when they stepped onto the other bank. It was only a short distance to the redwoods now. Eerie sounds erupted to their left, and Daniel gulped involuntarily.

Earnestly he asked, "Can you climb trees?"

The brothers nodded in unison.

"Quickly?"

They shrugged in uncertainty. They'd obviously never tried before.

"You'll have to! And you have to go really high, so nothing can reach you. Understand?"

They nodded again, their mouths tight with worry. Daniel could see the beads of sweat forming on their foreheads, and knew he was perspiring too. And it wasn't just from the moist air. He pointed at each boy in turn and then to a tree, indicating where they were headed and which ones to climb.

"Okay, when I say, 'go,' you run as hard as you can and

start climbing. Got it?" Daniel whispered. "Your life depends on it! I'm not joking!"

Daniel surveyed the surroundings, making sure as best he could that they would be safe venturing out. He couldn't hear the huge creature any more, but he was sure it was to the left of them somewhere. Before something else came into view, he decided it was as good a time as any to make their move.

"Go!" he whispered hoarsely.

He led the way as they raced across the open meadow to the redwoods. They dodged potholes filled with water, rounded a cycad, avoided lizards, and stopped short when a *Stegoceras* suddenly appeared in front of them.

"Easy now," Daniel said, holding his hands out towards the two-metre-long herbivore, who eyed him curiously. Quietly, he explained to Craig and Todd, "It's just curious, it won't hurt us, but go slowly."

With slow, sure-footed steps, they passed the *Stegoceras* as it twisted its thick dome-shaped head to watch them. Then it turned to forage the leaves of a small sycamore tree, and soon lost interest in them. They scrambled the last three feet to the edge of the redwood stand. Daniel pointed to the trees they should climb.

There was a sudden squawking of winged creatures lifting off from the forest.

"Climb!" yelled Daniel, as the ground suddenly trembled beneath his feet.

CHAPTER TWELVE

Without even thinking about it, Daniel clambered up the tree trunk, automatically searching for and finding toeholds and pulling himself upwards. Although he felt his arms and hands scraping along the bark, he didn't even worry about it. When he'd gone several metres, he looked over to where Todd and Craig were supposed to be. Craig clung desperately to the rough trunk of a tree, but Todd suddenly lost his grip and plunged to the ground.

"Quick!" Daniel yelled at Todd, but he could see the older brother wasn't good at climbing. He struggled to grab onto a low branch and brace himself against the trunk with his slippery sneakers. Daniel held his breath for a few moments, watching. His progress was too slow! Loud sounds reverberated through the forest. Something was approaching. Todd wasn't going to make it!

Although he was shaking, Daniel shimmied back down the tree and dropped to the ground. Then he ran over to Todd, who continued to struggle with climbing into the lower branches of the tree. Daniel saw the fear in Todd's eyes, and he motioned for him to try again. Then he gave Todd a heaving boost against his bulky backside, and at last Todd grabbed the branch and pulled himself onto it. Then he reached for another cautiously.

"Higher!' Daniel urged him, watching as Todd slowed down the higher he went.

The booming sound reverberated closer to them. Daniel didn't have time to run back to his tree, and Todd had stopped moving. Daniel followed Todd up the tree.

"Don't look down!" Craig yelled from high in his tree.

Todd looked down.

He came to an abrupt halt, clinging to the tree fearfully, not daring to move.

"Climb!" Daniel yelled at him.

Todd had only gone a couple of metres, so that even a small *T. rex* would be able to nibble at his feet.

"Move, Todd!!" Daniel pleaded, but Todd seemed frozen where he was, breathing hard.

Daniel had to do something!

The trees quivered as some monster beast advanced through the forest. Whatever was approaching was getting close! Without a moment to lose, Daniel grabbed a branch and pulled himself upwards behind Todd. He pried Todd's left hand from the tree trunk and placed it above them on another branch.

"Todd, climb!" Craig's shout pierced the air.

"You have to climb!" Daniel said urgently, and gave him a strong push that propelled them both upwards.

Suddenly a *Troodon* skidded to a stop below them! The deadly creature leapt towards Daniel, trying to grab his lower leg. Daniel screamed at Todd and gave him a powerful heave. The immediate threat below them seemed to release Todd from his terrorized stupor. Todd moved just in time for Daniel to swing upwards. The *Troodon* leapt again and ripped a chunk out of Daniel's pant leg before he managed to pull himself up.

"Faster," Daniel pleaded, shoving Todd and climbing with huge surges of adrenalin pumping through his veins.

All of a sudden, Todd skittered up the tree, well out of reach, faster than Daniel had ever seen anyone move before! Craig didn't waste any time either, going as high as he could.

Soon the three of them were a good seven or eight metres high, half-dangling from reasonably sturdy boughs. Daniel sighed in trembling relief as they caught their breath. Luckily, when the *Troodon* found he couldn't reach them anymore he had been distracted by a group of *Stegoceras* and had hastened off, scattering the small herd.

From where he sat, Daniel suddenly saw the school bus-sized creature from its front. It was a *Triceratops*! Harmless enough, because it was a herbivore, but still, it could have charged them.

As he clung to the branch, he dared to look straight down to the ground, and wished he hadn't. It was one thing to look far and away, but another to look below his feet from so high in the air. This was the second time he'd been so far above the ground, and it didn't make it any easier. At least he couldn't see a *Pterosaur* nest anywhere close by. All he had to do now was convince Craig and Todd to give back the strip of bark, and maybe they'd be fortunate enough to go home.

"Are you convinced this is for real yet?" Daniel asked. He could hear horrific screams and the sounds of a skirmish going on somewhere in the forest. The group of *Troodons* must have singled out a *Stegoceras.*

"Guess so!" Craig's shaky voice resonated from the redwood he was perched in some two metres way. "I think you're at least smart enough not to do something like this to yourself."

"What about you, Todd?" Daniel asked the older brother above him.

"You're pretty persuasive, Dino boy!" Todd said quietly, but his name-calling held a touch of respect.

Daniel suggested they rest for a few moments while he got his bearings. The Nelwins stared out through the forest at their strange environment, gawking in awe. They were sweating profusely and breathing hard.

"Have we really gone back into prehistoric time?" Craig whispered, turning with wide startled eyes towards Daniel from his tree a few metres away.

"Yes," Daniel answered, not wanting to say much for fear of alerting some creature to their presence.

Todd said in a croaking voice, "So no one else has ever been here before?"

"Just me, that I know of," Daniel whispered back.

"Wow, this is incredible!" Craig said. "Imagine! We're seeing something that nobody else has ever seen. Just the three of us."

"You sure do know how to get a thrill," Todd said, swallowing hard.

All of them remained silent for a few moments, staring out at the panoramic view of the forest and the sea beyond them. The ground still trembled with the approach of something huge. They weren't out of danger yet.

Daniel's thoughts turned to getting home. How would he get them all together with the bark? Plodding footsteps approached, coming closer now with the sounds of cracking branches and snapping underbrush. Whatever they did, they had to do it fast! He was sure the trembling of the earth came from something very big and ferocious. Perhaps another of Scotty's relatives!

He was also rather uncomfortable and sure could use a drink of water. Then he remembered he still had his backpack on and some bottled water. Did he dare drink any without offering it to the others? And if he offered, how would he get it to them? No time to lose! Quickly, he dug out his water bottle, took a few gulps, feeling the coolness searing down his parched throat. Then he stashed it away again. He needed all the strength he had to help get them home, especially as he was the injured one.

"As soon as it's safe, we'll go down and I'll give you some water," Daniel advised the two brothers, who complained strongly. That seemed to quieten them for a few moments.

Daniel peered about. He could see the mouth of the river again. Was it the same one from the last two times? Did he keep coming back to the same area? If it was, they must be on the other side of the forest from where he'd been on previous trips. He scanned about, looking for other familiar spots.

But suddenly, various birdlike creatures took flight, and Daniel knew a *T. rex* was near. Below he could also see small animals diving for cover. Craig and Todd noticed too.

"What's happening?" Todd asked anxiously. His eyes were wide and his voice high-pitched.

"I don't want you to freak out, but I think a *Tyrannosaurus* is just around the corner. They're really monstrous and they can swallow you in one chomp," Daniel explained to them. "Craig, make sure that you're as high as you can go. When you get to a safe place, make sure you have a good hold and that you won't lose your balance!" He turned to Todd, "Time to climb higher! I'll be right behind you!"

When Todd quit climbing, his white knuckles gripped the limb of the tree, and he'd wound his legs around it too. Craig's face was ashen, and he trembled. Daniel felt his whole body shaking as he recalled his previous encounters.

"This is going to be the one of the worst things you'll see," he told the others, "but once he's long gone, we'll get down."

Then he turned to Craig and with grave authority said, "Once we're safely on the ground, Craig, you'll give me the piece of bark and I'll try to get us home. Is that clear?"

Daniel sounded like he was speaking sternly to his baby sister Cheryl about not touching something, but the two brothers only nodded numbly. He hoped they understood how serious their situation was. All at once, there was a horrific crash and they all stiffened. The *T. rex* had arrived!

When it lumbered into view, Daniel thought Todd and Craig would drop out of their trees, because their bodies shook so much, not only from the vibrations made by the *T. rex*, but from terror. He prayed they'd keep hanging on tightly. The *T. rex*'s enormous head came into view first, its strong jaw hanging open to reveal sharp serrated teeth. It swung around quickly, using its stiff tail for balance and digging its two three-clawed feet into the ground for support. It wielded its head on a short muscular neck as it peered around for raw food with its ugly yellow eyes, with their stereoscopic vision, which Daniel knew meant it could easily see them.

All at once, it tilted its huge head with its demented grin upwards, and appeared to sniff the air. Daniel held his breath, keeping his eyes on the monstrous, scaly-skinned beast as it seemed to sense a different kind of odour. Probably human! No one made a sound, although at one point Daniel thought he heard some kind of snivel from one of the brothers. For a brief second, Daniel wondered how they liked to be bullied for a change. Then he turned his attention back to their major problem of the moment.

ROOOAARRR!!!! The *T. rex*'s terrifying warning reverberated through the forest ten times louder than a lion's roar, so loudly that Daniel covered his ears to keep them from ringing. Then the *T. rex* butted its head against the tree in which Todd and Daniel perched. Todd clung as if he was fused to it. Craig shuddered in the next tree, clinging desperately. Daniel found himself inching surreptitiously upwards. The tip of the *T. rex*'s head started to push through the branches right below him. His only thought was that he was likely going to die.

A sudden squawking of pterosaurs rose from afar, signalling the end of the battle between the *Troodon* and the *Stegoceras*. It also seemed to alert the *T. rex* that its dinner was about to be served in easy fashion. It plunged off at a fair speed, crushing small insects and foliage beneath its hefty clawed feet. Daniel thought he caught a glimpse of a scar on its hindquarters. Was it the same *T. rex* from his last trip to prehistoric time?

The noises of slaughter and its aftermath continued for some time, rippling over the forest. The main action, though, was far enough away that Daniel judged it safe to descend.

"Okay, you two," he spoke to them in a steady tone, meant to reassure them. "Let's get down now. Do it as quickly as you can!" Daniel started to descend as he talked.

Speechlessly, Craig and Todd obeyed, sliding down the last bit, anxious to have their feet on steady ground again. "Come over here."

They gathered quickly around Daniel at the base of his tree.

"Okay, Craig, give me the piece of bark, please," he said sternly.

Craig felt in his jeans pockets. Then a frantic look came across his face. He searched harder.

"I can't find it!" he barely squealed it out.

Daniel soothed him. "Calm down, Craig. You have to have it! Take a deep breath and take your time."

Sounds of disturbances were coming out of the bushes again. They had to hurry. Craig felt in each of his pockets, one at a time, and then turned them inside out. It was gone! Todd went over to help them, patting his brother down.

"What about the tiny pocket inside the right-hand one?" Daniel asked a little more desperately. The clamouring was getting closer, something was coming, and whatever it was probably wasn't friendly. It seemed to be coming at a fast-paced clip, as well, as if it were in a hurry.

Frenzied now, Craig sought the piece in the obscure pocket. A sudden look of relief came across his face as he drew the precious bark chunk into view. At the same moment, a *Dromaeosaurus,* a meat-eater with huge, sickle-like claws, raced down a path towards them. In the distance, Daniel could see several more, following the leader. They were ostrichlike in speed, and raptorlike in ferociousness. There was no time to lose. The creatures would be upon them momentarily.

Daniel grabbed for the piece of bark with one hand, making sure to keep in contact with Craig's hand, while reaching out and clutching Todd's arm with his other hand. Sure that he had a tight hold on both brothers, he gave a flip of his wrist and flicked the bark to the ground, just as the *Dromaeosaurus* sprang at them.

A terrible screaming split the air. It all happened so quickly, Daniel didn't know where the sound was coming from. Was the shrieking from the raptor-types, the Nelwins, or him? He felt himself falling to the ground in a whoosh of turbulent wind. Screams echoed around him.

Jed stood in front of them, joining in their screams just inside the cave as if they'd never left! Craig and Todd's traumatized shrieks died on their lips as they realized they were back in the present.

Everyone stood stunned, staring at one another with their faces frozen in mute terror. A moment later, Daniel sensed Mr. Pederson at his side and then felt himself being gently shaken to bring him out of shock.

"Daniel, can you hear me?" Mr. Pederson stared anxiously into his eyes, as if looking for a conscious response.

Bewildered, Daniel turned his glazed look onto Mr. Pederson and then around at the others, as if seeing them for the first time. Slowly he dropped his hold on Craig and Todd. Jed ran over to him and gave him a brief hug.

"I thought you were gone forever!" Jed stammered, thumping Daniel's back. "Where did you go? You just disappeared!"

Pederson put his arms around Daniel's shoulders and squeezed him in a bear hug. The old man's arms seemed to tremble. "I have to admit, lad, you gave us a bit of fright!"

"I'm okay," Daniel whispered hoarsely.

He still couldn't believe they'd escaped the terrible claws and flesh-ripping teeth of the *Dromaeosaurus.* The fierce, intense eyes of the creature would haunt him forever. He glanced over at the Nelwin brothers and saw them slide to the ground and lean against the cave wall. He'd never seen them so docile.

Slowly, the story came out of how Jed wasn't sure what to do, whether to stay or get help. In the end, he'd run for Mr. Pederson and they'd only just returned when the three boys suddenly appeared again.

"You look dreadful," Jed said. "What happened to you?"

Stuttering and stammering through his story, Daniel again felt the terror. He began with the first time he'd been knocked out and transported to the prehistoric world.

"I knew something uniquely extreme had occurred," Pederson said. "Something so real you were afraid to talk about it, and something you didn't understand or think was possible, but I didn't imagine for a moment it would be repeated."

"Why didn't you say anything before?" Jed demanded, giving his friend a slight punch on the arm.

"Because," Pederson answered for Daniel, "who would have believed him? Do you even now?"

Jed thought about it for a minute or two. "I guess it is hard to imagine it happened," he answered truthfully. "But I do know they disappeared somewhere right before my eyes, and look at his clothes! His pants are muddy and wet and his shirt is torn. It wasn't before."

Daniel looked at his attire. He'd already known about the pants, because they'd landed in the shallow lagoon, but the rip across the chest of his shirt came from something knifelike. He almost fainted when he realized how close he'd come to having his flesh ripped open. Then he noted the tear in his pant leg and gulped again.

"This time, though, he had witnesses," Pederson continued, looking over at the Nelwins. "Well, boys, how was your experience?" he asked with a slight twinkle in his eyes.

"Well, uh..." Craig started and stopped, totally lost for words.

"I didn't believe him at first, but..." Todd added and couldn't say any more.

"Do you now?" Pederson inquired.

Both boys nodded.

"That's the main thing!" Pederson said.

Daniel suddenly remembered Todd's accusations, and couldn't resist. "Okay, Mr. Pederson, I think we can turn off our DVD projector now!"

The Nelwins scrambled to their feet, abruptly indignant and angry. Pederson and Jed looked puzzled.

Daniel chuckled at the Nelwins. "Get a grip! You know it was real!"

Daniel explained to Jed and Pederson how the Nelwins had thought he was playing a trick on them.

Uncomfortably, the brothers slung their hands into their pockets and bowed their heads in embarrassment.

"It was incredible!" Craig said in awe. Then he turned to Daniel. "Now I think I see...I mean...uh...I can understand your interest in dinosaurs and stuff!"

"For sure," Todd agreed. "That was awesome!"

Daniel nodded. "I know."

"Something we'll never see again!" Craig's eyes widened in wonder.

"Let's hope not!" Daniel said.

Todd turned to Craig, "And *we* got to do it! Just us and no one else."

Craig nodded his head towards Daniel.

"Yeah, and Daniel, of course," Todd agreed.

"That was plenty enough for me!" Craig added.

"That's for sure!" Then Todd said to Craig, "Let's get out of here!"

"Just a minute," said Pederson, blocking the doorway. "We have a couple of things that we need to deal with. First, we have the problem of what you did last night to Daniel and to the Bringhams' property. Then we have to deal with what you've done here today."

Daniel had almost forgotten about the damage to his hideout. Both boys looked guilty and scared as they peered around at the shambles they'd made. Pederson and Jed stared in silent amazement at the destruction the Nelwins had caused in such a short time.

"It's up to Daniel what he wants to do about this mess." Pederson turned to Daniel then. "Daniel, do you think you can handle this part?"

Daniel nodded. Jed left the hideout to let Daniel work things out and waited patiently outside.

"I told the police what you did last night," Daniel said, eyeing them with confidence. "I'm surprised they didn't talk to you yet."

"Guess we weren't home," Todd shrugged his shoulders in more like his old attitude, then dropped his manner abruptly.

"Then how did you know I'd called them and they were looking for you?"

"We haven't been home since last night. We camped out in the hills," Craig said as if that answered the question.

Daniel knew this probably meant the boys were staying clear of their father and his latest binge until he sobered up. Now that they were older, they had figured out how to escape his violent rampages. Daniel also figured they'd seen the RCMP vehicle at their house and had been hiding.

"Well, I think you'd better contact the police and let them know where you are," Pederson said. "You know you can't get away from them, and there's no point in trying?"

They nodded in agreement.

"Now we need an apology," Pederson directed.

"Sorry, Daniel," Todd said, sincerely.

"I'm sorry too," Craig stated, shuffling his feet in the dirt.

"Well, that's a start!" Pederson seemed pleased. "But you still have the consequences to pay for the incident the other night."

Daniel interjected, secure in his demands, "And I want some sort of restitution for what you've done here today too! And I want my arrowheads back!"

"Please don't lay any more charges against us," Todd begged, handing over the arrowheads.

"We'll do whatever you like to make things better," Craig nodded morosely beside his brother.

"Well, for starters, you can clean up this mess," Daniel

instructed, righting his stump and sitting down weakly.

"Can we do it later?" Todd asked. "I need a rest. And we're hurt."

Daniel looked at the scrapes and bruises on the Nelwins and raised his eyebrows at them.

"You think I'm not?" he asked, pointing to his bandaged head, and the other marks on his body. "What you did to me hurts too!"

"Okay, we'll do it now." Craig agreed. He began picking up the pails and gathering the rocks. Reluctantly, Todd helped.

As they worked, Daniel groaned inwardly. He'd have to sort the stones all over again, but he wasn't going to complain for now. They'd never be able to figure it out. He removed his backpack and searched for his water bottle. When he found it, he took several big gulps, and then passed it to the Nelwins. They took it gratefully, before turning back to their work.

Abruptly, Daniel headed outside with a slight limp. Pederson followed him, and they stood with Jed at the entrance. They could hear Craig and Todd shuffling and banging around inside.

"Geeze, Daniel," Jed whispered, "how did you manage that?"

"I didn't give them a choice," Daniel said, grinning at Pederson.

Pederson grinned. "Good going, lad!"

"What else are you going to make them do?" asked Jed.

"Stay away from my place!" Daniel answered without hesitation.

They all laughed. Just then Todd stuck his head out.

"Is this okay?" he asked.

Daniel crawled back inside, leaving Pederson and Jed behind. He peered around, not saying anything at first. They'd put things upright again, but his belongings were still greatly disturbed, things were broken, and the dirt floor all cluttered with debris. Not only were they bullies, they were lazy!

"Well, this doesn't exactly look like it was." Daniel said.

"We can come back again later," Craig suggested meekly, realizing they hadn't done a good enough job.

"And I have a snakeskin at home. I could replace yours with it." Todd offered.

Daniel struggled with himself. Should he let them come back and mess with his stuff some more, or did he want to do all the work himself? Which would better teach them their lesson? Suddenly, he felt sore and tired. He needed to go home and lie down.

"Tell you what," he finally said. "You can go for now, but I want you to come back tomorrow morning with a shovel, a broom, and a garbage bag to finish it off. Be here by nine a.m."

They nodded, satisfied with the arrangement.

"What about the other charges?" Todd ventured to ask. "Is there any way we could do some sort of restitution for them too and have the charges dropped?"

Daniel stared at them thoughtfully. "You'll have to ask my dad about the damages to his property. He may let you work it off, but I can't say for sure. As for me, well..." Daniel thought again for a moment. Then suddenly he had an idea. "I could use some help until I'm healed."

For the first time, it seemed, the Nelwins actually looked at Daniel as a person instead of someone to taunt. They eyed him up and down, noting his bandages, and the cuts and bruises on his head and arms and legs. They seemed to realize for the first time how much they'd injured him.

"What do you want us to do for you?" Craig asked, sighing.

Daniel smiled. He still had chores to do, and now he was going to have help. He explained the situation to them.

"Fine, we'll be there at five," they agreed, reluctantly. Then they all crawled outside to join Pederson and Jed.

"Anything else?" Todd asked, sure there was more to come.

"You can't breathe a word about our trip to prehistoric time to anyone!"

"Who would believe us?" complained Craig.

"They'd lock us up on the insanity ward for sure!" Todd grumbled.

Craig asked, "What else?"

"I'll think about it and let you know later," Daniel said politely. "For now, let's go home."

"One more thing," Pederson said thoughtfully, stroking his chin. "What would you boys say to helping us out at the new dinosaur dig?"

"Could we really?" Craig's face lit up with excitement. Todd stood quietly by in obvious hopeful anticipation.

Pederson turned to the others. "What do you think, Daniel, Jed?"

Jed shrugged. "Okay, I guess. I'm just the new guy!"

Daniel thought about it for a moment, staring hard at the Nelwins, remembering the stalking and how much damage they'd done to him. Maybe it wouldn't be so bad to include them. Or maybe it would be a disaster and they'd do more damage. Did he really want them to be part of his paleontology world? They all waited for his reply. Daniel looked at Pederson, who said nothing. Then Daniel knew he had to give them a chance.

"Sure. I guess that would be fine," he answered, trying to keep the doubt out of his voice. He hoped that would mean they'd quit hurting him.

The Nelwins faces lit up with pleasure.

Craig asked, "When can we start?"

"After you've sorted out your problems with the police and Daniel's dad!"

The Nelwins nodded in unison and started heading across the hills.

"One more thing," Daniel called to them, remembering the most crucial thing of all. "This place is my secret place and I expect it to stay that way."

"No one will hear about it from me!" Craig shouted back.

"Nor me!" Todd promised sincerely.

"Okay, see you at the barn in about an hour!" Daniel turned to see Pederson and Jed staring at him in disbelief.

"Uh," Todd hesitated.

Daniel turned back.

"Thanks for the help climbing the tree," Todd said awkwardly.

Daniel crawled back into his hideout and dumped the contents of his backpack on the floor. He sorted out what needed to stay and repacked what he was taking. As he did so, he thought again about his adventure into the prehistoric world and about the injured *Edmontosaurus*.

Roxanne's skeleton and her nest had been found in what was once a riverbed. Could it possibly be Roxanne he'd seen? Was the river they'd crossed in the same place as the dig site on Pederson's land? Then he remembered the phone call about Roxanne from the Museum. Hadn't they said she had some bone breakage? Would the photos have been sent yet? He needed to get home to his computer.

Still thinking hard, he headed out to join Pederson and Jed, who offered to walk home with him. Mr. Pederson hoisted his backpack, and offered to pick up the cooler on his way home.

"I'm sure glad this day is almost over!" Daniel said, sighing. "I wouldn't want to go through any of this again." He was already trying to think of a cover story to give his parents for wrecking his clothes. Maybe by the time he got home, he'd also figure out how to explain the Nelwins coming to help him.

"You sure do get yourself into a mess of trouble, lad!" Pederson declared.

"I'll say!" said Jed, obviously happy to be heading home with his friend intact.

Daniel smiled at his friends and shrugged. "It's not as if I go looking for it," he said. "Besides, I think we've got everything under control now. No more problems with the Nelwins, we're ready for the tourists tomorrow. What else could possibly happen now that I got rid of that piece of bark?"

He took his backpack from Pederson and shifted it comfortably onto his shoulders. He didn't notice the small redwood cone sticking partway out of the flap of a side pocket.

"Let's go see if the Museum staff have sent us those photos of Roxanne yet!" He strode confidently towards home.

IF YOU WANT TO KNOW MORE ABOUT DINOSAURS...

I had a lot of fun writing *Dinosaur Breakout.* To make it as accurate as possible, I read many books and talked to experts like the real-life Tim Tokaryk. If there are any errors in information, they are solely of my doing, or they are ideas of my invention.

Please keep in mind that new explorations are always being conducted. This means that in the future you may notice some of the facts mentioned in this book have been replaced by new research information. Not all scientists agree about the significance of fossil finds and controversy sometimes exists until more research has been done.

Here are some dinosaur names and technical terms, along with their definitions, that you might find helpful. I've also included a Bibliography – a list of books and other sources that I consulted to help me write this book.

–Judith Silverthorne

VOCABULARY/DESCRIPTIONS

The material about paleontology found throughout this novel comes mostly from the Cretaceous Period. A brief description of some of the terms used follows, with their pronunciations. The Frenchman River Valley, where this story takes place, is located in the southwest area of Saskatchewan.

TERMS

CRETACEOUS PERIOD*(cree-TAY-shus):*
The Cretaceous Period, 146 to 65 million years ago, was the latter part of the Mesozoic era when great dinosaurs roamed the land and huge flying reptiles ruled the skies. A variety of smaller mammals and creatures also populated the earth and seas. The world was one of tropical temperatures all year round. Flowering plants and trees made their first widespread appearance, creating bright,

beautiful places with their reds, yellows, and purples. Before that time, there were only the browns and greens of trees and ferns and the blues of the skies and seas. NOTE: *Creta is the Latin word for chalk. The Cretaceous Period is named for the chalky rock from southeastern England that was the first Cretaceous Period sediment studied.*

CENOZOIC ERA *(sen-uz-O-ik):*
The Cenozoic era is the name given to the last major division of geologic time lasting from 65 million years ago to the present. The Cenozoic era is divided into two periods: the Tertiary, which began after the extinction of the dinosaurs about 65 million years ago until about 2 million years ago, and the Quaternary Period, which dates from about 2 million years ago to the present.

MESOZOIC ERA *(mez-uz-O-ik):*
The term Mesozoic means "middle animal" and was coined by John Phillips in 1840. This era is often referred to as the "Age of Dinosaurs." It is divided into the Triassic, Jurassic, and Cretaceous Periods. Dinosaurs, mammals, and flowering plants evolved during the Mesozoic era. All the continents as we know them now were jammed together into one supercontinent known as Pangaea, but in the middle of the Mesozoic Period, it began breaking up. The era ended with the K-T mass extinction.

K-T MASS EXTINCTION:
K-T stands for Cretaceous-Tertiary. "K" is for Kreide – a German word meaning chalk, the sediment layer from that time. "T" is for Tertiary, the geological period that followed the Cretaceous Period. About 65 million years ago, it is believed that all land animals over 25 kg (55 pounds) went extinct, as well as many smaller organisms. This included the obliteration of the dinosaurs, pterosaurs, large sea creatures like the plesiosaurs and mosasaurs, as well as ammonites, some bird families, and various fishes and other marine species. There are many theories as to why this mass extinction occurred, but many scientists favour the one of an asteroid hitting the earth.

TERTIARY PERIOD *(TUR-sheer-ee)*:
The Tertiary Period is the name for a portion of the most recent geological era known as the Cenozoic era, also known as the "Age of Mammals," which lasted from about 65 to 2 million years ago. The term *Tertiary* was coined about the middle of the eighteenth century and refers to a particular layer of sedimentary deposits. Many mammals developed during that time, including primitive whales, rodents, pigs, cats, rhinos, and others familiar to us today.

PALEONTOLOGY *(PAY-lee-on-TALL-o-gee):*
Paleontology is the branch of geology that deals with the prehistoric forms of life through the study of plant and animal fossils.

CREATURES

ANKYLOSAURS *(AN-kye-loh-sawrs):*
A group of armoured, plant-eating dinosaurs that existed from the mid-Jurassic to the late Cretaceous Periods.

BASILEMYS *(BAH-zil-emm-ees):*
A tortoiselike creature with a shell up to 1.5 metres across. This is the largest known fossil turtle from the Frenchman River Valley.

BOREALOSUCHUS *(BOR-ee-al-o-such-us):*
A crocodile in existence in the late Cretaceous Period in Saskatchewan. This crocodile would be little compared to its earlier ancestors, about two to three metres in length. It would be running from a *T. rex* as opposed to taking it head-on like the larger crocodiles.

CIMOLOPTERYX *(sim-oh-LOP-ter-icks)* ("Cretaceous wing"):
An early bird resembling typical shorebirds of today and found in the late Cretaceous Period in Saskatchewan.

DROMAEOSAURUS *(DROH-mee-oh-SAWR-us)* ("fast-running lizard"):
A small, fast, meat-eating theropod dinosaur about 1.8 metres (6 feet) long, weighing roughly 15 kilograms. It had sickle-like toe claws, sharp teeth, and big eyes, and lived during the late Cretaceous Period, about 76 to 72

million years ago. Fossils have been found in Alberta (Canada) and Montana (USA). A very smart, deadly dinosaur, it may have hunted in packs.

EDMONTOSAURUS *(ed-MON-toh-SAWR-us)* ("Edmonton [rock formation] lizard"):
A large, plant-eating member of the duckbill dinosaurs, or hadrosaurs, that lived about 73 to 65 million years ago in the Cretaceous Period in western North America. It had hundreds of teeth crowded together in the huge jaw, enabling it to eat tough leaves and other vegetation. This flat-headed duckbill grew to 13 metres (42 feet) and weighed 3.1 tonnes (3.4 tons). It may have had anywhere from 800 to 1600 teeth.

HADROSAURS *(HAD-roh-SAWRS)*("bulky lizards"):
A family of duck-billed dinosaurs that ranged from seven to ten metres (23 to 42 feet) long and lived in the late Cretaceous Period. They appear to have been highly social creatures, laying eggs in nests communally. Nests with eggs have been found in both Alberta and Montana. The only known hadrosaur in Saskatchewan is the *Edmontosaurus* (see description above).

MOSASAURS *(MOES-ah-SAWRS):*
Mosasaurs were giant, snakelike marine reptiles that extended 12.5 to 17.6 metres (40 to 59 feet) long. They were not dinosaurs, but were related to snakes and mon-

itor lizards. They were powerful swimmers, adapted to living in shallow seas. These carnivores (meat-eaters) still breathed air. A short-lived line of reptiles, they became extinct during the K-T extinction, 65 million years ago.

PTERANODONS *(tair-AH-no-dons):*
Pteranodons were large members of the pterosaur family from the Cretaceous Period. They were flying prehistoric reptiles, not dinosaurs, toothless hunters who scooped up fish from the seas.

PTERODACTYLUS *(ter-oh-DAK-til-us)* ("winged finger"):
A flying, prehistoric reptile, with a wingspan that spread up to .75 metres (2.5 feet); the wing was made up of skin stretched along the body between the hind limb and a very long fourth digit of the forelimb.

PTEROSAURS *(TER-o-SAWRS)* ("winged lizards"):
Flying reptiles, the largest vertebrates ever known to fly, they lived from the Jurassic to the Cretaceous Period.

PURGATORIUS *(pur-go-TOR-ee-us):*
A small, rodentlike mammal from the Cretaceous Period, which may have been about 10 centimetres (4 inches) long and probably weighed no more than 20 grams (3/4 ounce) and fed on insects. Probably this animal was named after the outcrops at Purgatory Hill in Saskatchewan where it was known to exist.

"SCOTTY":
The *T. rex* found near Eastend, Saskatchewan in 1991.

STEGOCERAS *(STEG-oh-CEER-us)* ("roofed horn"):
A bipedal, herbivorous, dome-headed, plant-eating dinosaur from the late Cretaceous Period about 76 to 65 million years ago. It was about 2 metres (7 feet) long and lived in what is now Alberta, Canada. (Not to be confused with a *Stegosaurus* [pronounced *STEG-oh-SAWR-us],* meaning "roof lizard," a plant-eating dinosaur with armoured plates along its back and tall spikes that lived during the Jurassic Period, about 156 to 150 million years ago.)

THESCELOSAURUS *(THES-ke-loh-SAWR-us)* ("Marvelous lizard"):
A semi-bipedal, plant-eating dinosaur with a small head, a bulky body, a long, pointed tail and short arms. About 3 to 4 metres (12 feet) long and less than one metre (3 feet) tall at the hips, the thescelosaurus could probably run at about 50 km/hr (30 mph) for an extended time. Recent fossil discoveries show that it had a powerful, advanced heart, which seems to indicate that thescelosaurus was an active, warm-blooded animal. Two partial skeletons have been found in Saskatchewan

TRICERATOPS *(tri-SER-uh-tops):*
Triceratops was a frilled dinosaur, a ceratopsian, from the

late Cretaceous Period that had three horns on its head. This plant-eater was about 8 metres (26 feet) long.

TROODON *(TROH-oh-don):*
A very smart, human-sized, meat-eating theropod dinosaur from the late Cretaceous Period. Fossils of *Troodon* have been found in Montana and Wyoming (USA), and Alberta (Canada).

TYRANNOSAURUS REX *(tye-RAN-oh-SAWR-us recks* or *Tie-ran-owe-saw-rus-recks)* ("tyrant lizard king"):
A huge, meat-eating theropod dinosaur from the late Cretaceous period. The largest meat-eater that has ever been, it stood 5-7 metres (16-21 feet) tall on its great clawed feet and had terrible, daggerlike teeth, 15 centimetres (6 inches) long.

OTHER REFERENCES & NOTES

BEES:

Over the past three years, Stephen Hasiotic, a Colorado University doctoral student and geology lab instructor, has found nests, almost identical to modern honeybee nests, that date back 207 to 220 million years, or about twice as far back as the oldest fossils of flowering plants. This means bees have been around longer than previously thought. The ancient bees could have found sugars and nutrients – which they find today in the nectar of flowers – in coniferous plants or even in animal carcasses.

RECEPTACULITES *(REE-sep-TACK- you-light-eeze):*

Referred to as the "sunflower coral" from 450 million years ago. At one time thought to be a sponge, it is commonly found as a flattened shape with a pattern of crossing lines like the head of a ripe sunflower. In more recent times, *Receptaculites* are considered spongelike rather than a true sponge.

CROCODILIANS:

Crocodilians are the order of archosaurs (ruling lizards) that includes alligators, crocodiles, gavials, etc. They evolved during the late Triassic Period and are a type of reptile.

DRAGONFLIES:

Dragonflies, primitive flying insects that can hover in the air, evolved during the Mississippian Period, about 360 to 325 million years ago. Huge dragonflies with wingspans up to 70 centimetres (27.5 inches) existed during the Mesozoic Era (when the dinosaurs lived).

BIBLIOGRAPHY

Bakken, Robert T., *Dinosaur Heresies,* Morrow, New York, 1986.

Gross, Renie, *Dinosaur Country: Unearthing the Badlands' Prehistoric Past,* Western Producer Prairie Books, 1985.

Lauber, Patricia & Henderson, Douglas, *Living with Dinosaurs,* Bradbury Press, New York, 1991.

MacMillan Illustrated Encyclopedia of Dinosaurs and Prehistoric Animals, Editors: Dr. Barry Cox, Dr. Colin Harrison, Dr. R.J.G. Savage, Dr. Brian Gardiner, MacMillan London Ltd., 1988.

McIver, Elisabeth E., "The Paleoenvironment of *Tyrannosaurus rex* from Southwestern Saskatchewan, Canada," NRC Research Press Web site at http://cjes.nrc.ca, 20 February, 2001. and Reference: *Canadian Journal of Earth Sciences* 39 (2002), Pages: 207–221.

Norman, David Ph. D., & Milner, Angela Ph. D., *Dinosaur,* Dorling Kindersley Ltd., 1989.

Parker, Steve, *Dinosaurs And How They Lived,* Macmillan of Canada, 1988. (Window on the World series).

Reid, Monty, *The Last Great Dinosaurs: An illustrated Guide to Alberta's Dinosaurs,* Red Deer College Press, Red Deer, Alberta, 1990.

Relf, Pat, *A Dinosaur Named Sue,* Scholastic, Inc. 2002.

Simpson, George Gaylord, *The Dechronization of Sam Magruder,* St. Martin's Griffin, New York, 1996.

Smith, Alan, *Saskatchewan Birds,* Lone Pine Publishing, 2001.

Stewart, Janet, *The Dinosaurs: A New Discovery,* Hayes Publishing Ltd., Burlington, Ontario, 1989.

Storer, Dr. John, *Geological History of Saskatchewan,* Saskatchewan Museum of Natural History, Government of Saskatchewan, 1989.

Tokaryk, Tim T., "Puzzles of the Past," *Blue Jay,* 52 (2), June, 1994.

Tokaryk, Tim T., "Treasures on the Shelves," *Blue Jay*, 52 (3), September 1994.

Tokaryk, Tim T., "Encounters with Monsters," *Saskatchewan Archaeological Society Newsletter*, February, 1991, Vol. 12, Number 1.

Tokaryk, Tim T., "A Tale of Two Vertebrae," *Saskatchewan Archaeological Society Newsletter*, April 1992, Vol. 13, Number 2.

Tokaryk, Tim T., "Serendipity, Surprises and Monsters of the Deep," *Saskatchewan Archaeological Society Newsletter*, October, 1996, Vol. 17, Number 5.

Tokaryk, Tim T., "A Paleo Breakfast," *Scotty's Dinosaur Delights*, 1995. Friends of the Museum, Eastend, Saskatchewan.

Tokaryk, Tim T., "Preliminary Review of the Non-Mammalian Vertebrates from the Frenchman Formation (Late Maastichtian) of Saskatchewan," McKenzie-McAnally, L. (ed) 1997, *Canadian Paleontology Conference Fields Trip Guidebook No 6. Upper Cretaceous and Tertiary Stratigraphy and Paleontology of Southern Saskatchewan.* Geological Association of Canada.

Wallace, Joseph, *The Rise and Fall of the Dinosaur,* Michael Friedman Publishing Group, Inc., New York, 1987.

URLS:

http://www.dinocountry.com

http://www.enchantedlearning.com

ACKNOWLEDGEMENTS

I am sincerely grateful to Tim Tokaryk, Supervising Paleontologist with the Royal Saskatchewan Museum (RSM), Eastend Fossil Research Station, for all of his expert advice, information, and suggestions; any inaccuracies are my own.

I extend thanks also to Harold Bryant, Curator of Earth Sciences (RSM), Mark Caswell, Executive Director of the Eastend Community Tourism Authority, and the T.rex Discovery Centre Staff; and a hearty thanks to Constable James Fraser with the RCMP satellite detachment at Climax for his invaluable information; and also to the residents of Eastend for their warm hospitality.

Thank you to Audrey Mark for a wonderful place in the woods to write, and to Brad Lane for his advice on mineral and oil rights information, and others on my journey who have supported me along the way.

As always, I appreciate the valuable team at Coteau Books, Nik, Karen, Joanne, Deborah, and in particular Barbara Sapergia for her insightful editing skills and Duncan Campbell for his fantastic layouts and designs.

ABOUT THE AUTHOR

Judith Silverthorne is the author of four previous books, including two novels for young readers. *The Secret of Sentinel Rock* won the Saskatchewan Book Award for Children's Literature in 1996. *Dinosaur Hideout* won the same award in 2003, and is a finalist in the Diamond Willow (Grades 4-6) category of the Saskatchewan Young Readers Choice Awards in 2004.

Judith has also written two books about Saskatchewan craftspeople: a biography, *Made in Saskatchewan: Peter Rupchan, Ukrainian Pioneer and Potter,* and *Ingrained Legacy: Saskatchewan Pioneer Woodworkers, 1870–1930.*

For more information about Judith Silverthorne and her work, you can consult her Web site at:

www.lights.com/writers/silverthorne